MW01166519

I wrote this book for my mother who has nobly battled against every challenge she's come across in her life.

Thank you God, Jen, Mark, Taylor, Eric Kimminau, and Lisa at Hear the Visions, without your support there'd be no book.

Special shout out to James Williams for being my artist.

Printed in the United States of America

(First Printed 2016)

ISBN-13:978-1532709159

ISBN-10:1532709153

Published through

Htv   Hear the Visions, LLC
           Sylvan Lake, MI 48320

Tournament of the Worlds

By *Travis J. Thompson*

Thank you so much for your support.

Travis J. Thompson

Prologue

Hong Kong, China

Saturday 06/06/16

11:30am

Bai stretched his arms out as he awoke looking up at the ceiling and let out a ravenous yawn. He strolled away from the king sized bed naked. His tattoo-covered skin seemed to radiate as the sun trickled in through the blinds, lengthy scars formed several trenches on his back and shoulders, wounds that had faded from the mind but not the body. Reaching for his studded black belt and designer dress pants slung over the mirror, he began to dress. Today, as every day, there was business he needed to take care of despite late night in the establishments of Hong Kong.

Bai finished adorning his blood red one of a kind Versace suit, rechecking every seam in the mirror. Bai was attractive by Chinese standards; strong, refined features made him look like he was a soldier. Though he came from a prestigious Chinese family, he was an outcast at a young age when it was made known that his mother birthed him out of wedlock. Having to switch from a luxury mansion outside the city of Guangzhou to the streets of Hong Kong, he did anything it took to survive, which paid off by the time his acceptance into the Wo Shing Wo Triad Organization at age fourteen. He was only thirty-three when considered the favored under-boss to one of the most powerful of the Triads in China, Boss Zhang. Zhang gave him permission to do whatever he pleased as long as it was within the territories of Hong Kong and Guangzhou. Bai slid on his last two pieces, his famous PM-9 latched into his left hip holster and a concealed Sabre slid perfectly onto his right side hidden by the suit coat. The sword, possibly the only thing he genuinely cared about was a gift from Zhang

as a sign of respect and honor.

Bai exited the elevator and the usual plump, cross-

eyed courier approached him with a black leather

backpack. Bai took it quickly checking the contents. By the

time he looked back, the boy was gone. Accelerating his

pace as he walked through the hotel lobby, all of the young

workers either bowed their heads slightly or looked away.

Looking directly in his eyes was a sign of disrespect, and

they all knew better. Hong Kong was his city, the hotel

was his home, and Bai set out to do what he did every day:

make money and handle his end of the business. He

stepped out of the hotel, shoving through the people traffic

that accumulated under the canopy for the valet service. It

was raining in Hong Kong, as it often did; the people that

forgot their umbrellas, huddled there attempting to stay dry.

Bai continued pushing his way through until coming upon

his white limousine that sat there naturally as though a piece of the street itself.

His newest driver, Chao, was a distant blood relative; he wasn't the brightest of men but came to Bai disgraced and in exile, much as Bai was. The window came down automatically; Chao called out formally to Bai who rifled through the stolen hard drives and several white bags filled with different narcotics. "Where to, boss?"

"Downtown, we need to meet with Detective Wang." Bai ordered and the vehicle began moving. Detective Wang was an undercover agent on Bai's tail for months, begging him for a confrontation, attempting to get pictures. So far, this particular agent had been unsuccessful, so when Bai had contacted him on his personal phone yesterday he had sounded aghast. Bai liked that Hong Kong knew he was out there running things, but what was the point of paying people off if agents followed his every move? His hotel was his fortress and if ever the day came that they raided it, heads would roll.

When they reached downtown, Bai looked around cautiously before shooting a text to the Detective their location from a burner he had pulled out of the backpack. A few minutes later a man with an umbrella too small to make a difference dressed in a black suit and tie approached, giving a small knock on the passenger window. Bai opened it and grabbed the man by the shoulder pulling him into the limousine and shutting the door. Chao drove off quickly and the vehicle swayed back and forth. "What was that about, I am an officer of the law?" Detective Wang questioned as he rolled out of the aisle onto the padded limousine seat across from Bai. The Detective was narrow and pale by Chinese standards, his glasses and hair were soaked from the rain, and he looked at Bai with his brow furrowed.

"You are a bothersome man Detective, stalking me as though I don't have enough issues already." Bai barked out dramatically, landing a punch to the Detectives shoulder; the man cowered and grabbed himself as his glasses slid down his nose.

"You pay the department but you don't pay me; I have a family to feed, I have bills to pay too!" Detective Wang attempted to get the words out with confidence while rubbing his shoulder. Bai would always discipline an officer this way if he had to meet with them face to face, to remind any enforcement who the boss really was.

"You are a pathetic man, nothing but a cockroach." Bai hissed the words at the young officer who began digging his hands into to his pockets. Before he could do anything, Bai planted his right foot hard into the Detectives shoulder pinning him against the seat.

"Right here Chao" Bai ordered, and the driver slowly pulled over halting the vehicle. Bai opened the door grabbing the Detective by the ear pulling him with authority out into an abandoned alleyway. In only a few agile movements, Bai threw the man onto the ground into a puddle, unlatched his gun aiming it at his chest. "You want a picture of me take a damn picture now." Bai burst out while moving his clinching his fists.

Reacting to where Bai was aiming pleadingly Detective Wang cried out covering his face, "Please no, don't harm me! I was wrong; I should have just let you alone!"

"If I ever see or hear of you again I'm going to break your teeth out of your face and send them to your mother! You understand me?" Bai announced before landing a definitive kick to his abdomen. Bending down, he picked up the umbrella. "Nice umbrella you've got here, is it yours?" Bai asked the detective staggering to his feet.

"Y…" he began to answer but looking back at Bai, knew the correct answer.

"That's right it's mine now, this city is mine. Don't you ever let me hear from you again," Bai told the man coldly. Bai ducked quickly back into the limousine in one fluid motion.

"Where to, boss?" Chao called once more through the cracked window.

Bai lit a cigarette and closing his eyes he inhaled an extra-large drag, "Take me to the north side to Suns so we can get rid of these drivers" he responded sternly, annoyed with the traffic. Fiddling with the small device on the limousines luxurious armchair, Bai cranked up the music attempting to drown out the thought of the dirty man he just dealt with. Bobbing to the rhythm of the music, he looked down at the phone to check the time; it was already high noon. He rifled through his pocket for his cigarette container and pulled out another of his imported Newport cigarettes.

The north side, Bai thought as they pulled down familiar streets, lighting the joint. He had done business there before, but not his primary spot for trade. As he opened the backpack to double check that all of the hard drives were there, he thought the black market wasn't as exciting as it was twenty years ago. Slipping into a daydream of memories as he inhaled another large hit then exhaled through his nose, he barely noticed Chao scream out wildly, until it was almost too late.

"Ahhhhhh Bossssss!" Chao screamed in a shrill, high-pitched voice. Bai tried getting a peek out of the window, but could only see a massive metal object come down with a wallop into the front of the Limousine.

Bai did not think but only reacted as he felt the vehicle launched into the air doing a hundred-eighty degree flip as the object demolished the hood. In milliseconds, Bai first opened the door then launched himself out onto the street. He did a commando roll hitting the ground hard, landing in time to see the limousine fall on its top.

The crowd around him screamed out, running and terrified, as he tried to refocus and shake away his daze to see what had happened. Bai's vision went blurry for a moment as he stood straight trying to see the object that had smashed down onto the limousine. He saw Chao slowly crawling out of the opposite side window, but then something monstrous caught the corner of his eye; it was something moving towards him. The crowd screamed in panic, a few unlucky by-standers flew through the air out of the behemoths path. The ground shook as it got closer to him and Bai could see a large metallic head lumbering along as people ran and screamed. The crowd finally cleared, and the beast began to slow down as it set its sights on its target, which Bai quickly realized must be him.

Bai could hardly make out whatever this was standing twenty meters before him but he knew it was not human. The vast amount of metal that formed a rigid plated armoring around its body suggested robotics however the way it hunched over and simply gazed in his direction gave off a feeling that Bai had never experienced, it was as if it was an evil spirit. Whatever it was it easily stood well over three meters tall and had a weight behind it that could lift a large car. The rain bounced off its massive armor, its red eyes glowed dreary light.

Bai didn't ask questions, instead unlatched his PM-9, and in a blaze of fury unleashed shots towards the armored beast. Each bullet deflected off the alloy hide or burst before impact, as if the machine had unnatural protection by some force field.

"What are you; some government robot here to finally put an end to my calamity?" Bai asked with authority.

The robotic monstrosity stretched out standing even taller with a path of green illuminating light seen around the jaw area circulating brightly and moving rapidly. Bai's eyes widened as a smooth and delicate Chinese woman's voice expelled itself from the being, "Congratulations Mr. Bai. You will represent your planet in the Tournament of Worlds. We will see you shortly." A large clicking noise shot out from the neck area and the robotic helmet the being was wearing folded on top of itself peeling back revealing a face. Bai stood in shock staring at the creature that appeared. It had a nasty, brown, wrinkled face, attached to a spheroid head that led down to a shriveled neck before disappearing into its armor. The sizeable red eyes that glowed bright ruby red stared at Bai burning a hole through his chest before letting out a blood-curdling scream that shook his core, something that rarely happened. Keeping his hands from trembling, Bai reached down to his sword, grasping the handle with temporarily weakened fingers. The creatures hand started to glow a royal blue color and made a crackling sound, the blue took form of a two-handed axe gnarled and pointed. It took a step forward. "Well if this is the end, so be it, I've got no regrets that I leave behind in this world." Bai shouted out to the beast, who was now taking another step forward. The ground started to rumble, Bai and the monster were on a collision course. Bai lunged leaving all fear behind and gaining resolve, putting all of his strength in the draw he made a desperate thrust toward the creature's unmasked head while yelling out. With the sword extended out about to make contact, the creature made his slash downward with the blue light weapon. The luminosity filled the street temporarily blinding all of those daring enough to watch. When the crowd came out into the street where Bai had met the strange creature head on, no trace remained of either.

Chapter 1: Secret Meeting

Washington DC, United States of America

Monday 06/08/2016

7:15pm

Eight world leaders representing very different regions congregated together around a rectangular, onyx marble table, hosting flat-screen monitors at each place setting. Sweat was visible on the Mexican Presidents brow; he fanned himself as he watched his screen staring with gloom. Clearly, there was an issue and it was grandiose enough to keep the most powerful people in the world on edge. Seated at one end of the table was the United Kingdom's Prime Minister Landon, a shorter plump, balding elderly male with a five o'clock shadow and a navy blue Presidential-looking suit and tie. He leaned over to his American counterpart Lady President Henderson and began whispering to her clandestinely, only to be cut off by Russian President Golov in his hoarse, thick accent, at the other end of the table, "We all agreed, no speaking until they arrived." Landon and Henderson focused their attention back to him as each of his fingers tapped simultaneously on the table as though to challenge the rest to speak against him. The Russian was the most daunting figure, standing nearly six foot four inches with the frame of a soldier and the cunning of an ex-soviet intelligence officer; he had been in power for a long time in a land where power was hard to hold onto. Before Landon built the courage to rebuke, Lady Henderson put her hand on his arm and gave him a look of agreement, and the room fell back into silence.

No further words were exchanged, but the men and women present all wore the same expression. War was imminent, but none of them could point a finger and place the blame on one another, so they sat anxiously waiting for the proper information to arrive. Most of the leaders kept their focus on President Golov, except Prime Minister Landon and Australia's ravishing newly elected female Prime Minister Lady Klem; the former who looked intently over at the elderly worried Prime Minister Nimitz of Germany; and the latter who seemed to stare blankly at her illuminated I Phone screen.

As if someone had summoned the dead the only door in the room opened, China's Prime Minister Feng seated next to Prime Minister Landon was so startled by the interruption, he spun so quickly in his chair to face the door he almost fell

3

flat onto the floor. In walked three suited individuals. Each stood side by side, as they paused at the door, taking inventory of the room. The first to move, a bald middle-aged Caucasian male that wore thick onyx framed glasses, led the group holding a briefcase that matched his outfit. He walked to the empty side of the table and took a seat at the middle chair. Behind him was a short and plump Asian female, her distinguishing feature a notable mole that protruded from the side of her cheek and ratty black hair pushed tightly to her head in a bun. She walked behind the middle chair and took a seat, huffing loudly from the apparently elongated journey she had made to get there. The last seemed to be of African descent, with a scowling look and skin so dark it was hard to distinguish it from his suit. Even in the well-lit room, his eyes popped out from his dark facial features. All of them wore the same stale look of intolerance on their faces and appeared covert as they gazed around the room at each individual. Considering the men and women already sitting down were some of the most powerful people in the world, any outsider would mistakenly think these three new arrivals were deities by the respect shown in silence that a pin drop would rupture.

"Ladies and Gentlemen, this is..." The President of the United States Lady Henderson began to introduce them attempting to take the lead, but the Caucasian man in glasses who she gestured toward cut her short immediately.

"No need for names lady President." the man addressed the leader of the free world sternly, taking off his glasses and setting them down, "Most of you in this room already know who I am, but during the time we spend together today, you will

5

address me as Agent so we don't complicate things." While Agent spoke to the group, he lifted his briefcase onto the table.

The President seemed taken aback as she and Agent exchanged momentary glances; before she could finally divert her eyesight elsewhere, she gave the man her nod of approval. A momentary awkwardness happened between everyone at the table. Golov broke the silence by clearing his throat and gesturing to the American leader, "How pathetic Lisa. You let your little dog bully you like this in front of your counter parts." The Russian scoffed with his thick accent.

"Ah, President Golov, I knew this would have to happen, so let me say this in your native tongue" Agent announced before speaking just as fluently in Russian. "Mr. President we are here because of a global security threat, not to measure strength or power. If you'd like to measure power, I can assure you the nations of the world that are in cooperation would pound your backwards country back to the Stone Age. I know you don't know me but I know you and this is how it's going to go: you are going to listen, with minimal interruption or I'm going to Taser and sedate you and your entire team stationed out in the hall, and then we will ship you back to Russia. You will wake up naked and cold in Moscow and you won't even remember we spoke. If I do that, you and your country are on your own. Now, I can't be certain that Russia can face this threat without the United States, or without me. I'm not called in if we think a million would die, I'm called in when there might be a billion or more casualties. Extinction, do you understand?" The room fell silent as Agent and the well-built Russian locked stares, and as President Golov's eyes had bulged further with each word that the man spoke; the other leaders noticed the fact that Agent had just disciplined him and a closed-mouthed mumble of approval left their mouths softly but without hesitation.

"Yes." President Golov finally muttered out, glancing around at the others, submitting to the need for cooperation.

"Great, let's go ahead and do roll call, we've all agreed we can speak English easily enough?" Agent asked the rhetorical question and only Prime Minister Feng seemed to nod along giving an answer. "Lady President Henderson, the newly elected President of the United States of America was kind enough to get everyone here and onboard." Agent introduced the most powerful woman in the world at the end of the table furthest from the door. She looked around at everyone else with her permanent scowl, wire-framed glasses, and bobbed hair cut; scanning everyone until her gaze fell on Golov again. "Though being the first female President to represent her country, she has been tough as nails in every crisis she's faced so far including the three most recent terrorist attacks." Agent finished introducing his apparent colleague.

"We all know the leadership representing Russia, President Golov" Agent motioned to the other end of the table.

Golov seemed to grimace at the sound of his own name and couldn't help but let out, "Do we really need these formalities this is serious business comrade?" No one responded and it was enough to stop the Russian from following up with another angrier question, though he was clearly already running low on restraint.

"Seated next to President Henderson we have representation from the United Kingdom Prime Minister Landon, and next to him President Feng from China; thank you for joining us personally gentlemen." Agent nodded his head at Landon and the two men locked eyes for a tiny moment, while China's President Feng put his hand up and introduced himself to the three suited figures.

"And next to President Golov we have Ethiopian President Asfaw and Prime Minister Klem from Australia." The Ethiopian man wore a khaki colored cowboy hat as well as a matching tan and white striped tie; it gave contrast to his dark blue suit and much darker skin. He looked up briefly before turning his attention to the black suited man across from him. Prime Minister Klem, who heard her name, looked up from her I Phone meekly giving a nod to the room, glancing around at the others one by one with her big cobalt eyes.

"Last but not least, in the middle of all of this chaos we have Mexican President Gomez and German Chancellor Nimitz." Agent could barely finish the introductions before President Gomez lost patience much like the Russian President.

"Senor with respect, President Golov is correct we must stop the charade, there is a global threat on our hands and we are sitting ducks; don't you understand?" the Mexican leader slurred the English out faster than could be translated and as soon as he finished the room erupted as each person began to argue with one another.

"Silence each of you!" Agent yelled out and the room went mute, each of them looked at him. "President Gomez we understand the situation and what we need to do now is share information. The

11

fact is we can't afford another outburst like that again, comprende?" Agent asked the man asserting his authority and President Gomez nodded in compliance. Finally having the room under some degree of control, he began by introducing the other two black suited individuals with him "To my left hailing from the Ministry of State Security in Beijing, Officer 47" Agent introduced the woman who sat to his left who still seemed to be struggling to gain her composure. She lifted a hand briefly to the room and let out a voice so innocent it could have hardly come from the woman that was there. "Hello" she purred to them. Agent looked at her before turning to his right, "To my right is African Union specialist head of the terror division, for the time being you call him Skellet. Special Forces Agent Skellet chose to sit rigid, fingers crossed and hands on the table. The whites of his eyes were the only color you could see on the man, but his eyes showed the dozens of fights he had been in; he was a tough man.

"Excellent, now that introductions are complete, let's begin. Officer 47 the floor is yours." Agent said while taking a seat in the leather computer chair.

Although Officer 47 was distinctively Asian, she blended in very well with the other two suited men, probably because they dressed and acted incredibly equivalent. 47 stood upon hearing her name, rifling through her briefcase efficiently. The rest of the room observed her pulling out a small tan folder and releasing a Chinese saying of relief under her breath. Opening the folder, she began walking around the room handing out an informational piece of paper to each individual. As she walked, she began to speak about the contents on the sheet.

13

"Bai Lo nicknamed big dragon, a man feared all around Hong Kong for any and every reason a man could be feared: laundering, auto theft, multiple batteries, mutilation, and we assume murder. Bai is a first lieutenant in one of the most feared of Triad organizations. He was from a prestigious family in China, but banished at a young age, which eventually led him to a life of organized crime in order to survive. We've busted him a few times but the charges never stick. He's got capable connections in the political scene that's for sure" she finished, giving the Chinese leader a challenging glance.

"Are you saying some petty thug is responsible for everything that has brought us here today?" the most senior in the room, German Chancellor Nimitz questioned Officer 47 with her heavy German accent as 47 walked pass. Chancellor

Nimitz had decided to wear a forest green dress suit; it didn't flatter her senior figure as she sat there slouched over in the chair looking at the sheet.

"No…far from it, Lady Chancellor." 47 stated, stepping around the Chinese leader's chair, handing him the parchment. "He has been living a protected life in Hong Kong for three years. Every now and then our informants get a glimpse of him on the streets, but for the most part he's stayed underground." Officer 47 was of Chinese descent, but spoke English as though she were born in the states.

Each person studied the sheet received from 47, peering at mugshots and every detail that the Chinese government could dig up regarding Bai Lo. His mug shot served as a portrait; his statistical information and photos taken by Chinese police profiling the Triad gangster did the man little

15

justice. 47 reached her seat again; rummaging through her briefcase, this time she pulled out a tiny portable hard drive and thrust it forward plugging it into the small device located on the table. The room's attention swayed from the sheet to each of the four sixty-inch flat screen curved monitor attached to both sides of the room. "So, shall we begin?" 47 exhaled the words before taking one last deep breath while glancing around the room, and delving into the story about what had happened in Hong Kong the day the criminal Bai Lo came face to face with something unknown in the bustling streets of Hong Kong.

"What, the hell--is that? Why wasn't I informed this had happened?" Prime Minister Feng burst out, exemplifying the fact to everyone that he had never seen something of the sort in his life. The rest of the room fell silent; it was the Chinese leaders first time seeing the images. 47 had switched to a picture the Chinese President didn't understand. He was looking at a metallic monster with a reptilian head, clad in a futuristic armor, wielding an electric blue energy weapon, and charging a Chinese man who was either dumb or brave enough to charge back with a sword.

47 responded, "As of now, we do not know. These pictures were taken by Bai's limousine driver, who claims it was a robotic alien that abducted Bai and spoke to Bai specifically, in perfect Cantonese." The room went silent again. Based upon the glances exchanged and lack of surprise, everyone realized what each person had in common. There had been similar instances in each country represented at the table.

"Remember, if the creature chose him, there's no doubt in my mind that we have not seen or heard the last of these things" Agent chimed in, cutting the silence. With his right hand rubbing his chin, he panned his view over each of the leaders to see the general reactions.

"Chose him? Chose him for what, death?" Prime Minister Feng voiced, he seemed shocked with a deep fear of the creature; further, surprised at the other leader's lack of empathy towards his countries situation.

"He is not dead, President Feng. He was chosen for reasons you and I don't understand yet" the black secret agent Skellet spoke out with a thick African accent. 47 clicked a small button on the computer and retracted her portable hard drive while Skellet stood announcing, "Ladies and gentlemen, there is currently one fact that's certain and that is these creatures aren't from Earth."

"Get to the point, señor!" The Mexican, President Gomez shot out slamming his fist down on the table, "What are they we are dealing with? Why now?"

Skellet gave the Mexican a cold stare but casually replied, "I saw one first hand. Fought against it as it tried to abduct someone; it was an alien, as the limousine driver reported."

The room became soundless once more, something that may have been the theme of the meeting, not so simple reticence. Skellet seized the moment plugging in his portable hard drive into the computer; an image popped up on all screens of an African Union Special Agent. He looked like he was in his mid-thirties and had an incredible amount of facial hair that lingered down his neck, balding man with a vertical scar running through his left eye, dressed in drab green and taupe camouflage.

He was holding a large bowie knife pointing it at the photographer. "This is African Union elite ghost unit Tesfa Wolde. He specializes in counter terror deep within areas where the African Union can't always get" Skellet explained. The leaders looked at Skellet with approval possibly comparing Tesfa to Bai Lo.

"Ghost agent?" Prime Minister Landon questioned as each of them studied the screen.

"Not any ghost unit either, this is one that had gone rogue a couple years ago and has gained a lot of press, he's been following his own doctrine in the public squalor of Kinshasa, Priest."

"Priest!" President Asfaw blurted out stunned, giving Skellet a deep stare.

"Yes, Priest" Skellet confirmed looking back at the Ethiopian President.

20

Chapter 2: Codename Priest

Kinshasa, Democratic Republic of Congo

Saturday 06/06/16

6:30am

Skellet walked down the road to a small hut, not knowing what to expect of the surprise visit he was making to his cousins home in the slums of Kinshasa. Along the streets were large masses of garbage and broken down cars, which made perfect playgrounds for the homeless orphans he could hear snickering and playing among themselves. The hut was fairly removed, every building seemed abandoned; only wild dogs and children dared to roam near. He wondered how Tesfa managed to survive in this environment for this long, two years in one of the hardest places on Earth. Priest, they began calling him last year, a vigilante. Skellet still didn't know what to think, other than him and his family had always had it tough and Tesfa had an even more difficult upbringing; it was the only explanation.

"Anton is that you?" a smooth sounding African voice revealed itself from the dark side of the hut. Skellet noticed the pin sized red light; as it caught his eye, he traced it down and realized he had a gun aimed at his chest.

"It is me, Tesfa" Skellet replied, putting his hands up as Tesfa appeared silently, with the G3 rifle aiming at Skellet's heart, and a large bowie knife gripped in his teeth. Tesfa looked wild in appearance, his eyes were blood shot from lack of sleep, and he had a long ragged beard that hung down to his chest. He wore a dirty white cotton tee shirt that clung to his toned physique from the heat, and blue jeans that were ripped and torn much like his worn out bronze shaded combat boots. Mud covered both his clothing and ebony black skin and there was a very visible crimson bloodstain on his shirt.

"In god's name Tesfa, you look like a wild animal" Skellet managed, after taking in the first site he had of his cousin in years.

Tesfa lowered his firearm. "Haven't you read the reports cousin, I am a wild animal" Tesfa said with a grin walking up to the astonished Skellet. Tesfa grabbed Skellet, pulling him into an embrace and doing his best to break the tension "Come inside and have coffee with me, we have a lot to catch up on."

"So tell me about the Priest," Skellet asked sitting in Tesfa's cramped dimly lit hut, sipping the hot coffee.

23

"You already know; it's a nickname given by some locals. I helped them" Tesfa began his story while pouring himself a mug.

Luvungi, Democratic Republic of Congo

Sunday 06/07/05 (10 years ago)

2:17am

Tesfa sat in the small, dark alley in the dead of the night; his goggles, skin, and beard blended in with the street, it was as though he was just another cardboard box of pile of rubble. He was waiting for it to happen; he knew it was going down tonight. He began to hear some dogs barking and knew the groups of men were approaching.

Tesfa watched as the eight men walked down the street and two large hungry pit bulls ran in circles around their feet snarling and nipping the air ravenously. They were local Boko Haram that Tesfa heard two days earlier plan this multi-victim slaughter as they had called it, in this neighborhood. These men also carried a reputation for past incidents, including hurting plenty of the youthful females in Luvungi. Tesfa wouldn't allow them to continue in his vicinity while he choosing his own assignments. The group reached the door, but it was too late. Two proximity mines went off that Tesfa had strategically planted earlier; he had figured they'd choose the most populated apartment building in this area for their attack. Springing to life, he jumped into action just as the explosion went off, he watched the two of the men, and both dogs engulfed in the flames. The front of the building didn't take extreme damage, some bricks fell on the surviving men, but for the most part, it went just as Tesfa planned.

He was sprinting with a combat knife in each hand, still unseen behind the partially fire charred men still reacting from the explosion. Tesfa reached the first before they even knew he was there. Tesfa thrust the blade with might in one of their backs and could feel his breath give out as he punctured a lung. Without hesitation, Tesfa threw the other knife into another man's chest that keeled over dying instantly, and then unshackled the first knife from the back of the other man. "Please, God have mercy" the last man screamed falling down next to one of the dead dogs and dropping his weapon; half of this man's face had been burnt off in the explosion. This last man was the leader; he was the one that planned this entire debacle, and the one who claimed to have tortured countless children in the fields. Bragging to the rest of these dead men and a bartender one evening while drinking, he

26

didn't know Tesfa happened to be at that same bar on that same evening. The civilians that lived in the apartment already started to approach Tesfa from a different alley; Tesfa had given them warning about tonight in case he wasn't enough to stop this group from doing what they came to do. Tesfa could see the dozens of children among the residents; still he had to finish this. "God would not show mercy on you" Tesfa replied throwing the knife deep into his chest, it met with bone and made an intense thump, the man fell backwards dead.

"You are a savior," a smaller woman cried out, it was a mother with two beautiful children trailing her every step; she approached Tesfa putting an impoverished hand on his shoulder.

"I am no savior, God is the only savior," Tesfa replied, looking down at the man he just killed.

Tesfa began to walk away but he could hear from among the crowd, an older man shouting out behind him, "You may not be any savior boy, but you will be our priest."

Kinshasa, Democratic Republic of Congo
Saturday 06/06/16
7:00am

"So you accept that you are Priest now? How many have you, killed just like those men Tesfa?" Skellet asked hesitantly fearing the answer.

"Five hundred and twenty nine" Tesfa responded with a cold unblinking stare. "They breed radicals in this part of the world Anton you know this" Tesfa followed up seeing the dismay in Skellet's eyes, but it was as though Skellet could see darkness in his cousin's soul.

28

"Cousin, I have been ordered by the Head of the Union to bring you back to Ethiopia, by any means necessary. There is a bounty on your head; you are viewed as a terrorist, at this point, in most of Africa." Skellet insisted. Tesfa put up his finger up to silence Skellet, diverting his gloomy disposition towards the door. "Are you listening? This is serious Tesfa, last night you blew up an entire..." Skellet tried reaching out again but noticed Tesfa was avoiding him all together.

"Shut up" Tesfa scolded with concern, sprinting up and getting behind Skellet before he could react wrapping his sweaty hand around his cousin's mouth, muting him. "Something is out there," Tesfa whispered in Skellet's ear before staring out the one tiny window. Skellet heard nothing.

Tesfa walked over with haste to the front

door grabbing his gun on the way. Tesfa held up the

customized rifle and kicked down the door with

force. Skellet got up quickly jogging behind his

cousins position. "Come out, I know you're there"

Tesfa shouted, his voice echoed off the brick walls

of the numerous abandoned buildings and for a

moment time seemed to stop in the heart of the

Kinshasa slums.

Nothing happened; "It was probably just the

children, cousin, you know how many orphans live

around here," Skellet muttered to Tesfa trying to

reassure them both, but Tesfa was stiff in his

position.

"It was no child," Tesfa replied giving

Skellet a powerful look of urgency.

Still nothing happened out in the street, there wasn't a single noise that they could hear that was extraordinary.

"Go inside, under the bed grab the AK" Tesfa commanded Skellet with an aggressive authority.

"Cousin, you are delirious and crazed," Skellet told him, peering outside for any sign of life that may trigger Tesfa to react like this. A thundering popping noise came out of nowhere from the sky; a flare followed it illuminating everything visible in a pea color for three seconds, and suddenly something was right where they both had been looking. Skellet didn't know what the metallic being was but it seemed to be looking right back at them. It was a medium-sized creature just a bit smaller than the average human but with long legs far out of proportion to the rest of its body and

31

tiny arms that reminded Skellet of the dinosaurs. It was wearing a glossy black armor from neck to toe giving it the appearance of an advanced robot, but where a robotic head should have been was an amber wool covered face with one white circular eyeball that seemed to be staring right at them. It had pointy ears that had several hooks piercings in them and stood up a foot over the top of its triangular shaped head. It appeared to be surveying the situation before grabbing its own leg and lifting it up into the air, mimicking someone stretching out before a jog.

"Go inside and get the AK, it's already armed with explosive rounds" Tesfa commanded Skellet quietly while they both took a military style step backwards while keeping the gun focused on the target.

32

A small path of green light was visible around the neck area of creature before traveling down the black armor and revolving around in a circle on its chest piece. Skellet seemed to freeze in place; it was only when noise came from the outside that he snapped back into reality. "Congratulations Tesfa Wolde. You will represent your planet in the Tournament of Worlds. We will see you shortly" an African woman's voice spoke in perfect English. Tesfa didn't hesitate after the last words came out; he unloaded the cannon in his hands. Shot after shot seemed to reach the target that stood perfectly still, but there was no affect. Tesfa ran out of ammunition, and stood observing the unmoving figure before him. The robotic humanoid stood in a cocky posture observing the hut contemplating its next move.

"You are an alien aren't you?" Tesfa whispered under his breath.

"What is it?" Skellet responded arriving back at Tesfa's side with the AK-47 aiming at the creature.

The foreign alien being squatted with one hand on the ground, while it's other hand extended behind and began to vibrate at an extreme frequency. Slowly, the pea colored light began to appear from the extended hand encircling it and becoming a ball of solid light. Both men looked at each other in confusion unknowing what would happen next. Skellet saw in the flash of a moment the eye fixated on Tesfa before springing itself up into the air like a spring.

Skellet watched as Tesfa reacted with savage speed and in two astonishing movements he had a grenade in one hand and he snatched the AK-

47 from Skellet with the other. He tossed the

grenade in the air directly in the robot alien's path

and shot it right before gravity pushed the creature

towards them. Tesfa ducked back shielding his eyes

and Skellet was fortunate to think the same. The

boom from the grenade deafened the entire area;

whatever had jumped at them burst into a ball of

flame crashing into the street below, barreling in a

hail of dirt that covered the entire street with a

massive dust cloud.

"What the hell was that Tesfa?" Skellet

yelled out slapping his right ear to try to get it to

stop ringing, he studied the area in the street where

it had crashed and half expected something to

appear from thin air again.

Tesfa propped the weapon up on his

shoulder in firing position, scanning the street like

Skellet for any life. Then as if a nightmare were

happening right before them, the creature walked out of the dust cloud towards them. The explosive rounds rang out as Tesfa unloaded but burst right before making contact with the creature. The robotic being didn't seem to notice the incoming fire; instead, it brushed itself off from the fall and stood at the edge of the dust cloud looking at them. Just as Skellet was about to let his guard down it made a blood curdling screech and bound forward towards them.

"It's coming Anton." Tesfa yelled releasing more rounds from the AK. Tesfa disappeared ducking into the house yelling on his way "Stay out here."

"What! What do you mean stay out here" Skellet yelled while simultaneously un-holstering his handgun and ducking behind some junk to shield himself from the creatures site. Skellet unloaded his handgun desperately hoping one of his shots would hit the mark but the robotic creature bent down once more. Skellet could see the jade energy clearly escaping from its hand, pulsating against the ground. It looked up at him with its one grotesque eye and made another screeching noise that echoed through the air. Finally, it sprung into the air again, jumping higher than any human could jump; a clear shot past Skellet, it crashed square through the roof of the house. Skellet spun around plunging through the remains of the door in time to see the alien and Tesfa on opposite sides of the meager space in a showdown. The alien had its green energy chiseled in the shape of a pointed spear and it was making a series of furious sounding clicking noises as if trying to communicate.

"Stay back Anton." Tesfa commanded staring the creature back in its eye. In the matter of a couple seconds, the creature made its move, a straight lunge for Tesfa with the spear. Skellet tried to shoot another round from his gun but he had run out of ammunition. Time seemed to slow down as Skellet watched the spear shoot out toward his cousin. Just then, with incredible speed Skellet could see the bowie knife whip out from Tesfa's right hand. It made a direct thudding impact with the creature in the middle of its eye sending it backward flying into chaos; squealing it stumbled back through the hut crashing into the wall and then the table they drank coffee earlier. Skellet raised the gun in his other hand attempting to place bullets into the creature, but the bullets disintegrated right before their eyes. The armored beast rolled around on the floor causing the only hefty decoration in the hut, a bookshelf that encased the far wall, to fall directly on top of it, and movement ceased. Skellet and Tesfa both inched forward as silence enveloped the room, Skellet could feel his heart pounding out of his chest.

"Do you think it is dead? We have to call this in now." Skellet advised Tesfa as they crept closer to where the bookshelf had fallen.

"I don't know, Anton. We should leave now. Either way, don't get so close to that thing, it is not..." Tesfa tried getting the words out, but before he could finish the bookshelf burst open in the middle, the alien appeared. Ripping the knife out of its eyeball, light blue ooze began to secrete from the wound, it clicked violently, and Skellet noticed the eyeball was still functioning even with the gaping wound.

Skellet couldn't react, before he knew it, the alien was next to him, and a green pike of energy was shooting unimaginable pain through his foot.

Skellet looked up at the ceiling and screamed at the top of his lungs. "Anton!" Tesfa cried out holding another knife up. Skellet saw the knife and expected to see the creature take another direct hit, but his cousin his face gave it away. Skellet noticed there was another sharp green object pressing up against his own neck. Tesfa looked Skellet in the eyes and said his last words on earth "For my blood." before dropping the knife onto the ground raising his hands in the air surrendering. The creature understood, and the green energy disappeared from Skellet's Adams apple then the creature pulled the other out of his foot.

"Goodbye Anton." Tesfa said looking his cousin in the eyes, as the alien kept the spear to Skellet's neck, preventing any movement.

In one flawless motion, the alien hurled the energy into Tesfa's chest. Tesfa disintegrated before

Skellet's eyes, vanishing without trace. No longer able to handle the situation Skellet damned his own life, as he tried to slash the creature in the face with his hand, but he swung at empty air. They were gone; Tesfa was gone.

In the secret meeting in Washington, D.C., the leaders stared at Skellet, unknowing what to say as the darker man's face stayed frozen as he thought about the incident.

"First a robotic dinosaur in China, now a one eyed alien bunny in Africa. These seem like bad children's stories." The Chancellor from Germany implied looking around slamming a hand down on the table gestural.

"Wasn't there an incident in Germany ma'am?" Agent asked the Chancellor lifting them all out of the thought of Tesfa Wolde.

Skellet turned and clicked on the small
button that 47 had held onto before. The screens
around the room came to life and a large one-eyed
face illuminated it; a precise sketch of the facial
features the alien Skellet had encountered was
hauntingly more surreal than anyone there
imagined.

"This is what we're dealing with; this is
exact information, everyone in this room has a
similar story?" Skellet questioned.

"A one-eyed alien bunny" President Asfaw
said in an alarmed voice while staring at the screen.

"Now then, President Golov, we have
reports that what visited Moscow didn't look like
either of these and showed incredible hostility in its
actions." Agent directed the room's attention toward
the Russian leader as he stood putting a hand on

Skellet's shoulder. Skellet sat as Agent looked at the Russian President.

"How would you know what happened in Moscow?" The Russian replied aggressively.

"This is a global security threat Golov. There's a reason we knew to contact each person in this room, and we have all the necessary information we just want you to share willingly." Skellet roared back, the emotions on his face were enough to get Golov going.

"If this is a global security threat, where are our Islamic allies?" The Russian stood firm this time observing each person at the table as he spoke, "Where are the French and the Japanese? And how do we not know if this is not just another American hoax or cover up?" he accused pointing a rigid finger at President Henderson.

"Countries without reported instances aren't currently involved Mr. President." Agent butted in before the American President cracked. Looking down at the table attempting to sway the most difficult leader into cooperation through diplomacy Agent added, "We are only trying to figure out what happened in each instance so we can all compare and share data Mr. President, this meeting benefits us all." He and the Russian President had a stare down before Agent finally reached into his front coat pocket and pulled out a small hard drive; as he did, Skellet undid his own hard drive from the computer. Agent plugged in the drive and clicked the mouse, a picture pulled up a mug shot of a man in his early twenties.

The room looked at Agent, "Who is this?" the petite blonde Australian Prime Minister Klem questioned. It was the first time she had asked a question among them; for the most part, she kept to herself observing her phone or listening vacantly.

"His name is Maximus Smith, born and raised in Detroit, Michigan. He served six years in the United States Army fresh out of high school; got high marks in everything before his first tour then a scandal involving a female officer in the middle of the desert got him a lenient early discharge. He didn't have a smooth transition when he got back to civilian life. Luckily, his father made a killing running several restaurants and nightclubs in the Detroit area during the recession; Max was running one of them. Presumably, both currently have close connections with some of the wealthiest and strongest roots in the city. Local police only make assumptions but the government thinks Max has gotten involved in something since returning" Agent opened up about the American.

45

All eyes in the room shifted from Agent falling on President Henderson who turned a different shade of pink due to unwanted attention; her only choice was to make a statement. "What? You act as if a Chinese Triad was any better. Every country has its valuable assets and every country has its rotten apples. What we do know is that he wasn't taken because of his activities here on earth." President Henderson caught each leader in the eyes before they turned their head back to Agent. Except President Feng who took the American leaders words insultingly, he gave her a cold stare.

Chapter 3: The American

Detroit, Michigan

Saturday 06/06/16

12:30am

The club was electrifying, the crowd packed in, everyone danced body to body, hot girls were grinding against drunken men who were buying getting them drunker, and Max loved all of it. He watched the crowd from his nearly vacant VIP lounge as another burst of smoke and florescent light rolled out from the stage, the women in the cages went wild kicking their legs and his bartenders were right on cue, no thirsty patrons tonight at Club K. This evening there was only one person in that crowd down there that Max was looking for. He liked to hide in the shadows, but Max saw him.

"Can we get down to business, Max? It's getting late for an elderly lady like me" a slender tan suited middle age African American woman with her hair curled and draped on each side of her face called out from the doorway leading to his private office.

"Yes of course, Detective" Max replied turning his head to the side revealing two large men guarding the doors. "Franky, Tony, go grab him. He's in the corner posted up by the round table on the east end." The guards briskly left the room without second thought.

"Are we going to, take care of him boss?" asked a shorter man wearing a sharp gray suite and matching fedora, pouring two glasses of bourbon across the room from Max.

"Please, don't talk like that in front of ladies, Lewis; I've scolded you for less." Max half mocked

48

his closest friend, spinning around with a devilish smile. Max was in his prime; standing six foot and weighing close to two hundred pounds, he had built his physique since childhood. His beaming blue suit and tie contrasted with his tanned skin and hazel eyes, but it somehow made his five o'clock shadow look clean cut. He walked past the female Detective, past Lewis to his small desk and began fiddling on his computer. He glanced at the two empty chairs across from his desk knowing they wouldn't be vacant for long.

"It wouldn't be the first time I've seen someone get roughed up here Max" the Detective remarked before accepting the glass from Max's associate Lewis and taking a seat on the only white leather couch in Max's office. Although the room was private it was equally as large as the VIP lounge and featured a fireplace, mini bar, and flat screen security monitor that most people could never afford to have.

"It won't happen today Camile, I promise" Max replied, glancing at his only friend Lewis and Detective Camile Holcomb from the FBI. He had known Camile long before he had left for and returned from the military; he never liked her, and thought Lewis shouldn't run his mouth so leniently. As he thought it, Lewis looked up and understood Max's expression. His friend began telling a reticent joke to the Detective that seemed to change the seriousness, if only for a moment.

One of the bodyguards burst through the door, both Lewis and Camile diverted their attention; it was Tony. "Max, I think we have a slight problem," he reported looking at each of them, Max continued on the computer as if not listening.

"Well, what is it, speak up?" Lewis asked abruptly. Max calmly clicking the mouse again, but he could hear the problem approaching.

"No! You know what…that is bull crap! I am getting through, too. He is not going to do this to me again…," a heavily drunken female voice yelled outside the door. Max instantly recognized who it was.

"I'm not letting you inside ma'am, I'm sorry." Max could hear Franky's rebuttal, but they could already tell she was getting in. Max heard every detail and he played it through his mind without having to see it. The pepper spray whipped out from her bra, the spraying fizz burning into Franky's eyes. He let off a piercing scream that seemed to blend in with the electronic music playing in the background.

The voice burst through the door as Franky clutched at his eyes. "You got a lot of nerve, Max" the beautiful bronze-skinned woman before them practically fell out of the tiny white club dress as she yelled across the room. Tony stepped forward and with one big bear hug grabbed the young girl before she could spray him too; Franky recovered and grabbed Max's intended target, a young man still waiting outside the door. Both bodyguards dragged the struggling, maniacal woman and the reserved young man across the room until they all stood before Max's desk as the two empty chairs.

"Jade, I didn't see you down there." Max replied to the woman who was now crying unable to break from Tony's masculine grip.

"Whatever Max, we only had one date and you think you can control my life now?" She screamed fiercely before her body went limp in

Tony's arms. Max paid no attention to her but instead stared ahead at the man Franky had clenched by the shoulder.

"Your name is Ryan, correct?" Max sat back asking the young man. Ryan seemed to be Jade's date this evening; he was a child compared to Max, it was shown on his unblemished face, maybe twenty-one or two, and he wore nice clothing, easily costing five hundred dollars, too nice for a kid his age.

"Yeah, who's askin'?" Ryan replied with a bit of Detroit ghetto slang, something Max always tried to prevent from coming into his club.

"What is going on here Max?" Jade blurted out trying to flail out of Tony's grasp to no avail.

"You need to watch who you're talking too dear," Detective Holcomb reminded Jade as she stood up from the couch and began walking over to them.

"Please, take a seat" Max commanded gesturing with an open hand to the chairs. Jade sunk down into the chair and out of Tony's grasp. Detective Holcomb walked up behind Ryan, putting a hand on his shoulder guiding him into the other chair.

"Ryan Martin, twenty one years old, Fraser Michigan, high school dropout, you've been selling stolen goods in my club." Max stated plainly looking at his computer.

Jade looked at Ryan "Whatever, Max you are such a liar" she interjected coming to life, but Tony put the paw of his hand on her shoulder and she was able to stay calm.

"It's true, Jade." Max looked at the young woman now with concerned eyes.

"Okay, so what? What do you want a cut of what I make?" Ryan questioned boldly looking Max directly in the eyes. Jade turned to Ryan with an exaggerated look of horror. Before she could say anything Max replied to Ryan.

"No, I want you to explain this," Max turned the monitor of his computer to show what he'd been looking at on his screen. Several local newspaper articles referring to a different case of questionable activity. The top article was the arrest of two teenagers for possession of high value stolen property.

"I don't know those girls." Ryan argued biting on the tip of his thumb. It was the sign that Max needed to know he was lying, not that he didn't already have proof.

"Really? Hold him down" Max countered. Both bodyguards grabbed each shoulder in one slick movement; Ryan was now restrained, bent face first onto the desk. Max stood with a vindication, he reached across the table and grabbed Ryan's hand spreading it out flat on the desk.

"Hey, what are you doing man!" Ryan protested wiggling, but the weight of both massive men holding him down kept him in place. In one hideous motion Max brought a modest sized hammer he'd been concealing, down sharply onto Ryan's exposed wrist. Ryan thrashed around in pain but guards kept a firm grip on him. Jade sat there in awe at what had happened so quickly, she began to protest but Max gave her a sharp look and she fell silent.

"Lie to me again and I'll do your other arm ten times over." Max stated coldly sitting back down. He viewed Ryan across the desk crying, and Jade, was in either a deep admiration or utter shock.

Max clicked on the computer mouse revealing pictures; Jade put her hand up to her mouth in a dramatic fashion while Ryan regained his composure. They were several HD images of Ryan selling to young women in the news article in Max's club, Club K. "You hustled these girls in my club; wo by the way is under age. You are using my place to run your market for stolen goods." Max explained smoothly.

"Max, may I leave? You can do whatever you want to him." Jade asked, glaring at Ryan who had gone from sobbing to whimpering.

Max ignored the question and instead continued to address the man who he'd just broken, "Ryan you're wanted by the FBI for grand larceny, sale of stolen merchandise, illegal importing. See the beautiful -- young, woman behind you? She is the agent that linked you to those girls and she was kind enough to come to me before reporting it to her office."

"Hello Ryan, I'm Detective Holcomb," the Detective playfully introduced herself patting the Ryan on the back.

"What the hell man are you a rat!" Ryan yelled out trying to gain his courage, he made a feeble attempt to break free but held down with authority.

Max stood up again with even more speed than before, he raised the hammer in the air with the same dramatic fashion. Both Ryan and Jade shrieked but Max kept the hammer cocked giving Ryan the look of death stares. Ryan breathed heavily below him expecting Max to bring pain down onto him again. "She is Detective Holcomb, she is a reasonable human, and for a price, Detective Holcomb can link these girls and the thefts to a guy named Bobby who resides up in Roseville; who's known for hurting little kids but hasn't been caught." Max continued his speech. Both Jade and Ryan stared at Max in confusion; neither of them understood what was happening.

"What?" Ryan questioned, the man had stopped crying, but his face had become red with humiliation and discomfort.

"See my friend Franky behind you, the one who has your right shoulder? You are going to go with him tonight down to Detroit and pick up something for me. If you can do that, without running your mouth or giving him a hard time, you will work for him for a time unloading delivery trucks and other odds jobs, without pay. Three times a day you will check in with Franky. If you don't do this, Detective Holcomb will find you and throw you in prison; I will guarantee it. Do you understand?" Max explained doing his best to clear the confusion on the matter.

"What if I refuse? You just broke my arm man" Ryan mentioned meekly, he had lost any semblance of the former Detroit accent. Max simply raised the hammer up and smacked it down hard on his desk; everyone in the room seemed to jump besides the bodyguards and Lewis. "So, when do we start?" Ryan tried turning on the desk so he faced the man pinning him in place, whose eyes were still puffy from the pepper spray.

"Right now. Let's go get your arm fixed up" Franky informed him, grabbing him by the shoulder the bodyguard pulled him up and lead him hastily out the room.

During this time, Max had gotten into a stare down with Jade. He casually ordered the rest of the room "Alright, business is over. Camile, Lewis,

Tony; I have unfinished business with my other guest, if you could leave us." Camile looked at Max and rolled her eyes as Lewis escorted the detective out of the room.

Lewis and Tony stood at the window in the empty VIP lounge watching the dance floor. The beat was jamming and the dance floor seemed to part as an incredibly lively dancer sprung forward and a crowd formed around her. Lewis was fixated on her; he'd never forget how she moved as the crowd parted like the red sea. She was wearing an incredibly shiny outfit; the crowd reacted to her as she moved around elegantly spinning and jiving to the beat. Lewis had felt so mesmerized he barely realized the woman had an elongated metal cylinder object strapped onto her back.

"Hey, are you listening to me boss?" Tony asked Lewis again, this time waving his hand in front of Franky's eyes, "I told you, you got to clean up the office this time. I cleaned up last time."

"Hey, look at her down there, Tone," Lewis had phase out what Tony was saying, he pointed to the dancer that had the entire clubs attention, Tony turned his head to look. The big bodyguard reviewed her from head to toe as the rest of the crowd was doing. She wore formidable spiked metal combat boots that went up to her knees; her bare skin was visible from her thighs to her butt and must have been painted dark purple. From her butt to her head she was clad in the same spiked metal armor as her boots. Lastly, she wore a Spartan like metal helm that covered most of her lime green curly hair; a plastic attachment to the helmet covered her face giving her a mercenary like appearance. On her back was strapped a futuristic assault rifle, it didn't diminish that alien look

62

whatsoever and the crowd began to notice the dangerous accessory. She moved rhythmically as she danced as though it was her first and last time ever dancing.

Tony knocked on the office door violently before opening it. "Max we need you now, there's an issue," Tony panted frantically.

"Yeah, I'll be out in a minute; have Lewis handle it" Max replied

"Max!" Tony yelled back. Max looked up at him, none of his guards used his first name unless it was vital, let alone yelled it at him. Max followed Tony into the VIP lounge as Tony began to explain "I looked several times boss, but it isn't like anything I've seen before."

The crowd roared cheering as the female moon walked around in a circle, bouncing at the end of her walk and shaking her rear promiscuously

63

against an admiring bystander, the man went into

frenzy giving his closest friend a high five as she

stepped away. Max caught just a glimpse of her

and he instantly saw the assault rifle on her back,

her purple painted skin, the lime green wig, and the

metallic plated clothing. Max walked out of the VIP

room onto the spiraling staircase leading down to

the bar mumbling to himself "Damn." The music

became much louder out here but it was one of his

favorite songs, his club only played the best

electronic dance.

"Hey!" Max yelled out to the nearest

bouncer while pointing at the woman, "I want her

out of here she's causing a commotion" The

bouncer lifted his hand to his ear, gesturing he was

unable to hear the words.

Max watched as the body of another

bouncer, one of his heavier African Americans,

64

suddenly flew through the air before connecting with the wall. The music suddenly cut off, Max turned his attention to the dance floor where a woman screamed out, and the crowd began to scatter. Another bouncer cut through the air, and this time Max saw the culprit, the one behind all this was the woman he was trying to throw out; she looked past the people surrounding her and straight at Max. Max's right hand Lewis was harassing the female dancer with the weapon, yet keeping a safe distance from woman while ordering the other bouncers to grab her.

A pulse of red light blinded him for a moment as he stared at her pondering who it was. Then he noticed there was a thin red line of laser, scanning his body, and it was coming from the woman's helmet. He saw her expression go from unsure to a wide grin, until one of the bouncers made a lunge for her and all hell broke loose.

A rapid spin and hard palm thrust to the bouncer's chest was all it took to send the grown man flying almost like a cartoon, much like the other two men before him. Max watched as Lewis tried directing another of the security staff as he attempted to grapple the woman from behind. She head-butted him violently with her helmet and he fell to the ground in pain grabbing at his nose. She turned again to face Max, this time she looked agitated.

"Stop" Max hollered approaching the woman, he didn't want to see another of the bouncers make an attempt at grabbing her and fail. Max was trying to understand what the woman's intentions were, coming into his club and roughing up his men like this.

66

Then she spoke loud enough for him to hear and with a voice that was out of this world, it sounded as though she was underwater as she growled each word with a strong effort, "Maximus Smith, you have been chosen and must come with me now." Max looked confused; it felt like he had stepped into a movie. Before he could reply, she undid her rifle and the room turned bright red. Max saw his outstretched hand as it began to disappear in the net of crimson that shot from her cannon.

"We've questioned every person in the club; none of them believe that the woman was a human being." Agent explained to the room back in Washington, "Also after Max vanished, it seems this female alien disappeared at the exact same time."

"What exactly are we dealing with here Agent?" President Henderson questioned sternly.

"Well, the representatives from Russia, Mexico, Australia, Germany, and The United Kingdom all have similar stories Lady President." Agent replied looking around the room at each leader as he named their country, they provided a slight nod proving that he was accurate. "What we know so far, is they're alien, none of them seem to have the same description, they're gathering individuals who will represent our planet in some type of tournament, and an invasion force landed here on our soil at approximately the same time, apprehending all of these individuals at once."

Chapter 4: The Tournament

"A tournament" The Russian President repeated looking at the rest of the room.

"Why don't you tell us about your incident President Golov?" President Henderson prompted.

"How do we know this isn't a new Chinese experimentation? You Chinese with your little robots" Chancellor Nimitz questioned the room with a bigotry that came out of no place in particular. She scowled at President Feng as the room went silent, leaving the Chinese leader no choice but to respond.

Feng blurted out "The Chinese people have acceptable relations with most countries in this room and the largest policy my administration has followed is no foreign intervention"

"The German people as one are very saddened by our loss, we lost a hero!" The German Chancellor Nimitz articulated the words in her best English as she continued looking at the Prime Minister with her sagging eyes, her cheeks wobbling back and forth and one frail finger pointed at him.

"We don't really know the man that was taken from Gold Coast; we're still missing a lot of information, I've been trying to get what we have here as soon as possible" the Australian Prime Minister spoke to no one in particular, possibly attempting to find her voice at the table or change the flow that had become hostile.

"Yes, well we are happy they took Catalina, the black widow. She was a wanted criminal and a plague within our country; but we need to know what to say to our people, how to keep covering up what happened in Mexico City..." The Mexican

President sat with his arms crossed, scoping each

one of them before directing his glare back to

President Henderson. Only the Special Agents kept

their composure. They didn't intervene in the

arguing this time; instead, they opted to let it die

down before beginning again. In all diplomatic

affairs, banter would frequently arise especially

among these people. The fact that everyone had

contained himself or herself until now seemed

remarkable.

Then a frantic knocking at the door snapped

everyone out of the critical state. Agent lifted his

hand up to a tiny device in his ear and whispered, "I

understand, send her in."

The room's attention swayed from the door

back to Agent, wondering what could possibly be

happening. A middle-aged woman with frazzled

dark curly hair and blue eyes, wearing a white lab coat and thick black glasses entered the room. Agent undid his hard drive and the woman stood taking her place at his side, choosing to stand.

"Hello everyone, I'm Stacey Switzer." She waved to the room, paying extra attention to President Henderson who Stacey seemed to be in admiration of.

"What did your team find?" Agent asked the woman bluntly. She inserted her drive into the port of the computer.

"It's not good. We thought at first it was just some basic cosmic noise, but we're positive now it's a message relating to Max's incident"

"A message" President Feng repeated looking around, his eyes widening as he looked at each leader. His focus ended on Chancellor Nimitz who gave him a cruel glare.

72

"Yes, let me show you." Stacey replied. An audio file appeared on the screen. Skellet, who was still holding the controls, looked up at Agent who looked over at President Henderson. She nodded her head and Skellet pressed the small button.

"Earth, I am Ra." A haunting, deep voice came out of the speakers, "Master of the Galactic Federation of Trade, Hospitality, Entertainment, and War."

A rambunctious static noise broke off all sound for a second before Ra came through clearly again. The people around the room listening to the message looked at each other amazed, unbelieving of what they heard, even Agent looked concerned.

"We have not made a visit to your desolate planet for over 2,000 human years, but this year, the dwarf planet you call earth has been selected for the Grand Tournament."

Another sharp noise broke in, everyone winced, and Agent couldn't help but mumble aloud "In perfect English, I can't believe this."

"We are currently orbiting Earth on our mothership Platform and will make contact..." The obnoxious noise seemed to cut off the transmission and prematurely end the message, but Ra managed to get a few more words that made their way through the static, each of the leaders looked one another bewildered. "The Tournament will decide the fate of your world, much like it did long ago" Ra finished before finally disconnecting. Stacey promptly stopped the recording to avoid hearing the wretched sound again.

"Ancient mythology, a lot of this stuff is starting to make sense now." Skellet started the conversation, looking up at Agent, who was rubbing his chin inquisitively.

"What is that supposed to mean, you are referring to the Egyptian God?" President Asfaw asked each leader mimicked staring a hole through the African agent.

"It could mean that we've just been spoken to by what is known as the ancient deity, Ra. Worshipped as a Sun god in Africa during Ancient times," Skellet explained to the room, each of them absorbed the knowledge.

"Or we've just heard a super intelligent alien-being speak in our language! They've been here before, they're in orbit above us, it's all disturbing," Agent rebutted, returning Skellet's look.

"President Golov, we've got mixed reports from Moscow. Maybe the key to revealing the true nature of this tournament and that message is within the information we already have in the room" 47 spoke up wisely, interrupting the others thoughts and continuing the meeting as planned. Agent gave Stacey a nod, and she departed as quickly as she had arrived.

"The men that have been mentioned so far don't compare in importance to who was taken from Russia" President Golov stated, his suspicious eyes wandering around the room.

"That is your opinion President, but if we wish to work together you will relay to this room what you've been told." Skellet angrily mentioned while burning a stare through the Russian that suggested the man should speak up.

"Alright, I will tell you what I personally saw." Golov responded, feeling the rooms ears lock in on his speech as he finished the words.

Moscow, Russia

Saturday 06/06/16

8:00am

"Gummy Bear, Oh Gummy Bear..." A young woman called out as she entered the mansion's front door walking past the posted guards dressed in all black. The slender woman stood taller than most at five foot ten inches, her blonde hair swayed around her cute freckled face as she walked angelically through the home with her tight black skirt and loose white blouse slightly open in front. Up the glowing spiraled stairs, she ascended and into the great hall leading to the masters chambers, she entered. The statue-like bodyguards throughout the mansion watched as she walked past. Although in extravagantly lit surroundings, she still radiated like the sun. Her body pressed and swayed showing how tight, but curvaceous her body was beneath her

77

clothing "Where are you my gummy bear?" The woman purred, nearing the massive brown oak doors leading to his room. Portraits of past Russian greats like Peter and Catherine stared at her, as she got closer. The final two bodyguards posted directly at the door parted giving her space, and as she approached, she slowly pushed it open. "I bet you are in here" she greeted him smiling while walking through the door.

There she was, his girl, his spy, his Special Forces Hacker-Lucya. She was the definition of beautiful and could easily make any man's heart melt, she looked like a Victoria Secrets model, and her outfit did her slender curved frame justice. Russian president he may be, but to her he was only Vladimir. Channel 1 played on the curved television, every realistic detail jumped out on the screen. He smiled and asked as she approached him, "My love Lucya, how has Syria been?"

"Rebels, Rebels, Rebels, Vladimir. When will we show real military progress in the region? I swear, it is like our great leader is really a cynical man with so many women to please he cannot lead this great country of ours." Vladimir struck a match and lit the half-burnt Cuban cigar in his mouth while she pranced around the room until reaching him.

"Cynical? …You little tease!" Vladimir jested with her as she spun around the room to see what he was watching.

"You know you love me Vladimir, much more than you love these silly reporters" she commented turning to face him and putting her hands on the end of the bed, "You wouldn't have kept me around this long if you didn't love me, besides I'm the best hacker you got old man."

The Russian President chuckled deep in thought. The reasoning could be much simpler. "That last part is surely the truth." He suggested with cold eyes staring at the television, before letting out a fabricated laugh.

In the flash of a moment, the laughter stopped for them both as Lucya snapped her head to the side, changing the mood in an instant. "Did you hear that?" she asked him. Vladimir listened carefully, unable to hear anything but the television in this large room. Before he could say anything, she reached her finger to his lips with one hand. This made him very upset, but before he could protest, she sprang to the door. "You may want to run Vladimir," she put in before yanking the door open and bolting down the hall. Before he could say anything in protest, a massive entity crashed through the side of his wall, shaking the entire room violently and causing multiple pieces of furniture to fracture and explode.

"What the Devil!" Vladimir croaked out looking at the massive creature, then at the damage to the wall. The armored beast easily stood over twelve feet in height and was clad from head to toe in a dirty yet durable plated metal armor. Neon green lights seen streaming from its head region were spinning circular around the mouth and eyes. The creature stood stretching out towering over any other object in the room; it was recovering from the jump it made through the wall.

"Fire! Protect the President," the guards shouted while running into the room guns blazing. Golov stared in horror at the creature as it turned its glare to him. Its shape was that of a jumbo

81

rhinoceros but stood on two fat stumpy legs, its head was more rectangular and a metal jaw line revealed a mouth wide enough to swallow the television whole. President Golov pressed himself hard against the bed unmoving as it began to let out a massive roar so loud it knockcd both guards backwards sending them to the ground. One could hear the numerous guards approaching from the hall but all shots fires reflected off the armored hide. "The bullets aren't doing anything," another guard cried out from the hall, shooting at the creature. The alien turned its attention from the President to the hall and in a single bound launched itself forward knocking the guards in separate directions as it leapt past them.

Golov snapped back to life as the creature exited, "After it!" he yelled out to the confused guards attempting to recover. The entire house shook as the creature jumped from the hallway downstairs, cutting of Lucya's retreat. Golov watched as the creature blocked the door; its head began glowing while the green light circulated around its mouth area as it got in a stare down with Lucya.

"Congratulations Lucya Konstantinov. You have been selected to represent your planet in the Tournament of Worlds. We will see you shortly." It declared in a young Russian woman's voice. Everyone stared at the behemoth including Lucya frozen in her tracks. Vladimir reached the hallway to see the creature staring at the young woman down. A sharp popping noise that came from the creature's helmet broke the startled silence. A slit across the metal eyeball area seemed to fold back on top of itself, revealing a dark colored leathery head with grey blotches of furry skin. It had yellow diamond shaped eyes with dark black pupils that scanned around the room frantically as it breathed heavily from what appeared to be only slits instead of a nose. It roared, and the noise seemed to come from the slits instead of any mouth.

"Shoot it now" Golov cried out to his security staff who had been staring with bewilderment. They released a hail of fire below, but it was too late. The creature lunged forward with extreme propulsion, given its smaller legs. With one swipe of one of its massive paws that radiated a fluorescent vermilion, Lucya was gone and with her the alien.

"I stood there in shock...no sign of either of them. We surely thought, given her profession, it was the CIA or even PSIA but after hearing the transmission, there is no doubt we are dealing with a highly sophisticated group of alien beings" the Russian President finished the story as he gestured at the other leaders, who seemed surprised that he

had revealed so much. Golov was not a man for

flare, or lies. He certainly wasn't a man who shared

intelligence without a lot of effort. "Instinctually, I

knew it had to be an alien, I mean none of us

possess that technology yet" he finished and looked

at President Henderson who nodded at him.

Chapter 5: Black Widow

"The one that showed up in Mexico City had a face like a demon, how do we not know that isn't the end?" Mexican President Gomez spoke up asking each of them, and the room's attention fell upon him. "We got reports; images from the hotel surveillance system where she was abducted. No colossal body, but it used some type of power and brought half of the St. Regis Hotel down, it killed 147 people" he sounded at them as he got more riled up with every word, "The people want answers. I can't give them anything like this."

"You need to share with the room what you know. We have all of the images of the creature; is there anything else you can tell us?" Agent looked at the Mexican leader, prompting him to share his information as the others had

"Yes, Catalina Gonzalez", President Gomez began, "As I mentioned before, she was a con artist, a professional thief and a seductress."

Mexico City, Mexico

Saturday 06/05/16

11:00pm

Catalina pressed the man hard against the hotel door and smothered him with her smaller frame. Standing only five foot two was not an issue as long as her cleavage was bursting out of her dress she maintained perfect control. She pressed her lips against his neck and could see the first trickle of sweat run down the side of his cheek. The man pleaded with her "Let me unlock the door, baby please, tonight I am all yours." He turned quickly and slid the card with a trembling hand through the security lock. As the door cracked open, stepping inside he attempted to flick the lights on. Before he could find the switch, Catalina kicked him in the back and he fell to the ground tumbling forward. "Why?" he managed to get out as he tried to recover on his hands and knees before she kicked him hard across the face.

She was a Mexican bombshell, an enchanter; that's how she survived and she was proud of it. The men she ripped off associated themselves with the cartels, they were predators like her; except their prey tended to be helpless and usually wound up dead. Catalina's sleek medium cut black hair rested on her shoulders perfectly as she finished tying the man up with the steel wire she had stashed away in her velvet black purse. Her perky chest, tight rear and natural luscious lips with matching dimples gave her the perfect advantage in her line of work The dress she had worn to seduce petty underboss Juan of the Gulf Cartel was startlingly promiscuous, the poor man hadn't had a chance. Sitting on the bed reading his credit card information off aloud to tease him, buying item after item as he lay on the floor hog-tied. "Oh, this one is two thousand, I wonder if you can afford it" she remarked smiling clicking the buy option and looking back at her guest wiggling around on the floor frantically. "OH! This one is so pretty." She laughed, holding up the credit card punching the numbers in on the laptop again. The man on the ground squealed as she spent thousands of his dollars in moments.

Then, something was wrong. Someone snuck up on Catalina; no one had done that since she was five. In the closet, someone was hiding in that dark place. Catalina could feel their breathing and sense a creepy malice. She stopped and stared

90

intently, waiting for an armed hit man to pop out, waiting for a machete boy to try another assassination, her hand dropped down to her side gripping the silenced Russian Ot-s38 revolver and automatically unlatched the weapon from her outer thigh. Waiting in anticipation, she stared into the blackness of the hotel closet. Juan lay in silence as well, possibly sensing the same thing. A neon light glowed for only half a second and Catalina let off 3 muffled shots into the center of whatever made the illumination. For a brief moment as the gun flashed, Catalina could see a figure standing there. The lights formed a circular motion in the dark and rotated rapidly. "Congratulations Catalina. You will represent your planet in the Tournament of Worlds. We will see you shortly." A Mexican boy's voice called from the dark.

"Come out here little boy, I will not hurt you." Catalina called to the figure that stood in the shadows, raising her gun towards the green circular glow. A popping sound came from the closet, it sounded like a tube releasing air pressure.

Catalina noticed out of the corner of her eye Juan wiggling on the floor had gotten his feet and his mouth free somehow. He looked up at her saying in a panic "We need to get out of here now!" as he finished the words, an eerie and dreadful noise began in the closet, whatever was there seemed to be laughing through the two nostril holes. Catalina looked back at the closet and could see small black eyes looking at her from the darkness.

"Heh ha ha ha heh ha ha" it sounded like hideous, forced laughter; as each syllable came out the eyes would bounce up and down. Catalina smelled something foul and looking back to Juan

92

realized the man had pissed himself. She quickly to

a dive downward to his side and helped him wriggle

his feet free. Catalina got up and ran, flying

through the door while Juan sprinted right behind

her. They ran down the hall as fast as they could.

Behind them, a frail creature with a tubular body

that extended down to the ground hiding any feet.

Its exposed face looked bumpy and hardened like

bark and two hollow beady black eyes and an oval

shaped black gaping mouth, slithered out into the

hall.

"Run" Catalina cried to Juan unable to

fathom what it was chasing her. She was able to

glance back but only for a second, she witnessed as

a gooey bright yellow energy dispelled from the

creature's mouth shooting out at them, grabbing

Juan by the foot.

"Help me please!" Juan screamed, Catalina didn't stop running but was able to see the man out of her peripherals as he shot backwards sliding on the floor. She turned in time to see the creature's mouth expand out, unnaturally, as it sucked Juan into its mouth a foot at a time. Catalina turned again as she made it to the end of the hall but froze in place hearing Juan's bones snapping and crunching together; horrifying screams came from Juan as he was being gnawed to death by the creature.

She turned realizing the screaming had ceased and the only sign of Juan having been there was a pool of blood that formed underneath the creature; that was looking at Catalina. The being reared its large head back and let out a terrifying screech surely alerting everyone on the hotel floor. By the time the creature looked forward toward its prey though, Catalina was gone. She had slipped into the ceiling at the end of the hallway, hiding, observing the creature through a tiny slit where a light met the tile. The creature glided down the hall to the single door leading to the stairs. It looked wildly in every direction, turning to check behind itself. Catalina raised her gun, aiming at the creatures head as it paced in a circle below her confused. It raised its bark face in the air and Catalina could hear puffing noises coming from the bead like nostril holes; it was sniffing. Done sniffing, it looked at the door near the end of the hall and began to make the same laughing noise. "Heh ha, Heh ha ha ha ha, heh heh heh ha" the sounds came out hauntingly. The creature was motionless as it continued laughing which made it even more frightening to watch. Catalina got the impression that it was about to bolt out the door. Instead, it stopped the laughter and shot a glance straight up at the ceiling where Catalina was perched near the crack. She made eye contact with the creature and it let out another shriek as the shimmering yellow substance shot out of its mouth at her. The impact with the ceiling barely redirected the creature's projectile, but it was enough for Catalina to make a quick dodge. She raised her gun and shot at the creature's face through the hole it created, unleashing four bullets that seemed to dissipate right before they made contact with the creature's eyes, but one bullet managed to penetrate and go into the creatures open mouth. The yellow energy vanished, and the creature lunged backwards falling against the hallway wall howling on the floor, grabbing at its face.

Catalina jumped down to the hotel floor and began sprinting toward the opposite end of the hall towards the elevator. Hearing the noise, hotel guests began popping their heads out into the hallway, mumbling as they came out and screaming as they saw the creature writhing on the ground. Catalina bolted past all of the chaos, just as she always had. Reaching the end of the hall where the elevators were, she pushed each button. Every elevator was currently above her, but one was only two floors away. Catalina turned back toward the creature noticing the hideous noises had again concluded. The monster was standing hunched over itself, coughing up purple liquid onto the ground. She turned back to the elevators to check progress, but it was too late, the yellow goopy tentacle latched around her leg, yanking her to the ground.

Catalina tried grabbing onto that which had wrapped around her tightly, but her hands burnt with a fiery sensation and she yelped out for help while trying to dig her fingers into the ground, her nails cracked on the tiled hotel floors as she was dragged foot-by-foot back to the being, seemingly to be eaten alive like Juan.

An angel, or more likely a shirtless cartel bodyguard covered in Los Zetas tattoos with a thick black mustache wreaking of alcohol snuck up behind the creature and slammed it in the back of the head with a baseball bat. The tongue that previously protruded from the creature's mouth wrapped around Catalina's leg disappeared and the alien fell over sideways slamming into the wall where this time it lay unmoving. The man beat the creature again in the back with the bat until the wooden object splintered into a thousand pieces as it decimated itself on the creature's metal hide.

"Are you okay?" her large savior asked approaching her from behind as she got herself up. Catalina pressed herself tight against the hotel wall looking at the unconscious creature, tears rolled down her face; she nodded at him as he approached but the man quickly grabbed her hand to inspect her burns. Other people had poked their heads out of the hotel room doors and were observing as her the man asked her "what the hell is this thing?" tilting his head at the monster that lay on the floor.

Catalina trembled in fear as she glanced at it again "I do not know" she replied hesitantly; usually men associated with the gangs were not this kind. The elevator chimed, and the doors popped open, Catalina was still recovering but she stood erect looking at the doors which would take her to true freedom, "I'll be leaving now" she told him while mustering up the rest of her courage. Turning her body toward the elevator, she tried to break free from his grasp but he clutched onto her wrist tight.

"I don't think so, Black Widow" the man marveled leaning in; she could smell the tequila on his breath as he gripped tighter.

"Do I know you?" she asked trying to get her hand free but he pushed her in place.

"Oh come on you know who I am baby, everyone knows who Big Mig is," the man told her mockingly leaning in even closer, "I'm Miguel Ricardo baby, Los Zetas for life." he whispered tightening his iron grip on Catalina's arm.

Catalina looked back at the man, even more tears swelled in the sides of her eyes. "Please don't do this" Catalina wept as she submitted, but the man raised his fist at her in a threatening manner.

"No, a trashy woman like you doesn't get to beg" he replied. Catalina could only look the man in the eyes, maybe she was sick of running, and maybe she was finally defeated. "There's a million dollar

100

bounty on your head lady. If you don't know who I am I bet you would know me after that reward," he stated cocking his fist back. Catalina put her free arm up to protect her face; it was her last and only defense. Before the man that saved her could begin beating her, a yellow electrifying spear burst through his mouth and shot past Catalina head, smashing through the wall. The man's eyes began to bleed a dark red, and a witness screamed at the end of the hallway before slamming the door. Catalina adjusted her focus to the creature as she felt the man's grip on her wrist ease up. A dinging noise behind Catalina snapped her back into reality; the elevator door had popped open again, without a second thought Catalina turned running as fast as her petite legs could move her. The creature began making its hideous laughter noise, the entire hallway began to shake; Catalina realized she wasn't

101

going to get away and the energetic substance

coming from the creature wrapped around her waist.

Catalina could not move. Everything around her in

the hall began to crumble; she only had a moment to

look at her own hand as it disappeared into the light.

The leaders meeting in Washington, DC

looked at the screens; seventeen of the top floors of

The St. Regis Hotel in Mexico City cut in half

revealing the effects of an explosion. The next

images of Catalina and the creature in the hall,

taken moments before the destruction took place,

held the entire room's attention.

Chapter 6: German Officer

"Well, you've done a superb job hiding this mess so far" The German chancellor chimed in looking at President Henderson, who brushed the comment off giving her attention back to President Gomez who got further flustered.

"The world can't be kept in the dark so carelessly, not everyone has accepted the cartel story" President Gomez commented.

"But no doubt you've received support from all of your allies at this table" Prime Minister Klem assured him.

President Gomez responded, "The internet is already buzzing with rumors, aliens included."

"Which is why it's so important we put together the remaining pieces of the puzzle, ladies and gentlemen" Agent butted in while fiddling with a pen. The room turned its attention to the man who had stayed calm through most of these stories.

"Lady Chancellor?" 47 questioned the eldest woman in perfectly fluent German, "We all received the same intelligence indicating the situation that happened in Berlin was a more peaceful exchange. Is there any truth to this?"

"First of all, my sorrow goes out to all of the little brown people that lost their lives; as you know our country has had difficulties adjusting to your people in the last couple years, so I didn't mean to sound disrespectful" the Chancellor responded ignorantly; the others only stared at her.
"Lady Nimitz I believe you're getting confused, this is President Gomez from Mexico and your disrespect can't be masked, some people are who they are." Agent corrected the woman while trying to maintain civility. Chancellor Nimitz looked at the

Mexican leader while rummaging around in her front chest pocket, finally pulling out a tiny flash drive. "One of these creatures appeared and took one of Berlin's finest police officers, without force. I'd say compared to most of you we've had the biggest loss in this room," she informed them.

The Chancellor slid the flash drive across the table to Agent. He swiped it up handing it to 47, who quickly popped it into the drive. "What's his name?" President Golov asked the Chancellor.

"Her name -- is Konstanze Nimitz, not that she would mind you calling her a man, she is queer as the queen of the fairy people but I love her anyway, she is my favorite granddaughter" Chancellor answered. Agent clicked open the first image saved on the hard drive. It was a head shot of a stunning woman, with dirty blonde hair and thin lips that frowned but led to a sculpted round chin.

Her hazel, almond shaped eyes surely burned a hole through whoever photographed the image.

Berlin, Germany

Saturday 06/06/16

5:00am

Leon had been Konstanze's partner going on seven years but somewhere down the line, things had gone sour between the two of them, as they usually never spoke. Chaz, their Shepard companion, sniffed around in the back seat as he moved back and forth anxiously; the only noise his partner seemed to permit came from the canine. Konstanze was his opposite in every aspect; she was the top of her graduating class while he barely managed to pass the tests. Nicely tucked into a black suit and tie, she wore better than most men did, it was obvious she had a frame built for finesse.

While Leon, known to be a klutz, continued to put on weight even through extra exercise and dieting. Konstanze had family connections that reached all the way up to the very pinnacle of the German ladder; Leon had no living family besides his cat Greta, and his cat hated him. In every way, she was ideal of beauty, built and stacked; Leon wasn't even average looking, his oversized nose, and chubby cheeks always turned pink during the cooler months. He was balding, could not afford a hair transplant, and he hadn't seen his own feet for months due to his bulging gut. Konstanze was his same height but weighed one hundred pounds less; she was muscular but not beefy, skinny but not weak. Maybe Leon's own envy had ended any hope of being friends.

"Right here" Leon said pointing down a side road. Konstanze nodded squinting, turning the wheel of the blue and silver Streifenwagen sharply; Chaz shifted in the backseat to look out the window at the passing homes. This was probably the only reason behind their partnership, Konstanze had insisted that she work the immigrant cases herself, and Leon knew these streets, he called them home since he was a kid. They made it to their destination within a few minutes of silence; as they slowed down Chaz began to whine in excitement realizing they arrived. The refugees that came from the Middle East had a difficult time adjusting in these neighborhoods but for the most part, there hadn't been issues. Leon hadn't had any personal troubles with them and he called several families of them neighbors; but every once in a while they'd get a tip of a child gone missing, or an aggressive man beating a woman in public.

"Remember, no getting physical with these

people they probably don't speak a lick of German. One female and two males but there may be kids there" he panted the words stepping out of the car. He had a gut feeling that his words had fallen onto deaf ears as Konstanze ignored him, letting Chaz out and walking past him quickly. They arrived at the door and she knocked three times as instructed by their source. From the porch, they could hear the people inside reacting. People shuffled and a man yelled out to someone in Arabic, the aggression in his tone made Konstanze draw her Taser. Leon looked over at her in disgust, he already knew what was going to happen next, and nothing he could say would stop it. Konstanze knew there were probably children inside, but that would not stop her from doing what she was intent on doing. Leon unstrapped his own handgun "It doesn't have to get ugly like this every time, this is the reason you have a Taser and I have my gun" the lecture from him came out of routine. When the door opened, all hell would break loose.

The door creaked open and a woman draped in a black burka looked out at them with dark eyes and began to greet them in Arabic. Konstanzc pushed her to the side and moved past before she could finish a word; storming through the door her Taser came to life with electricity.

"Damn it" Leon grumbled as he followed behind her. Leon entered the home and watched as Konstanze's pin shot across the room into an unsuspecting man's chest pumping ten thousand volts of electricity into him and dropping him like a stiff board. "Infidel we have done nothing!" another man dressed in all black from head to toe shouted, running into the room with a knife from a hallway. Leon lifted his weapon but hesitated, Konstanze

110

delivered a debilitating sidekick to the man's sternum; Chaz followed her act tackling the knife wielder to the ground.

"You know this man?" Konstanze asked straddling over the squirming middle eastern man, showing him a picture of their real target, child kidnapper Firas Maloof.

"No way will I tell you anything!" the man shouted in half German but enough for them to understand. The heel of Konstanze's boot wandered to the man's junk, it did not take him an elongated amount of time after, to squeal. Leon watched in disarray but couldn't act surprised; they had a good tip that this family housed Firas and a few of his hooligans.

"Okay I'll talk" the man cried; Konstanze snapped her fingers and Chaz let go of his bite bouncing back and barking loudly. Leon began to put the other man in cuffs as he watched the interrogation, as he'd grown accustomed to her tactics. While the woman Konstanze knocked out when they first entered remained unconscious next to them Konstanze bent down putting a knee directly on the man's chest.

He whimpered more and gave in, "He has the girl that you've been looking for. They are headed to Prague at this moment with plans to escape to Turkey." The man Leon was holding wiggled fiercely as he regained control of his muscles, but Leon brought his weight down stopping any hope of moving.

"Idiot they will kill us! We have done nothing wrong!" he gasped the words in pain as Leon crushed him.

Konstanze shot a sharp glance over at them, "You're lucky you aren't dead anyway, how much time on reinforcements?" she asked in vanity, knowing they would be there any second. Dulder and Freza walked in the door dressed identically, they were rookies compared to them Konstanze and Leon, but enough to get these three down to the station. Konstanze lifted her hostage up by the back of his arms with ease; her strength was incredible. "Take it from here boys," she told the two uniform officers. Leon lifted up the man he was handling, who began struggling again; the captive stomped his foot down hard on Leon's, making him lose his grip only for an instant; just long enough for him to bolt toward the kitchen. Not fast enough for Konstanze, who had gotten behind them and clothes lined the man to the ground.

"You didn't have to do that I had it" Leon attempted covering his mistake as they walked out of the house and back to the car as Chaz trotted

113

behind Konstanze in sync with her steps. Although she was beautiful with a pedigree upbringing, Konstanze reminded Leon of a German Shepard because of her strength, cunning and prowess when it came to work. If Chaz were human, he would probably be her perfect partner. They climbed back in the car awkwardly. After situations like these for over two years, they both knew she wouldn't get in any trouble for breaking minor violations like those she just did. Her Grandmother is the leader of all Germany, and her current girlfriend Kass is one of the major powers within the Chancellery.

Leon reached down to grab a cigarette and lighter from his pocket. She hated when he smoked but permitted it when she violated rules. He started up the car. She looked forward rolling her eyes away from him; that's when she spotted Chaz outside, cradled in the four metal arms of a creature

114

with violet-jeweled eyes. "Chaz!" Konstanze screeched out jerking back. Leon looked forward seeing the being and the lit cigarette dropped from his mouth onto his lap. It was robotic in appearance, standing at least ten feet tall with long skinny metal legs and four arms that led to three fingered miniature hands stroking the German shepherd, which it held like an infant. Konstanze got out of the car faster than Leon had ever seen her move at the same time reaching under the seat, drawing a firearm, and aimed it at the colossal being.

Leon trembled as he got out of the car, unlatched his gun, and drew it also aiming at it. "Put the dog down" Konstanze yelled out at the creature assertively. That seemed to shift its attention from the car to Konstanze and a loud popping noise came from the creature's shiny metallic helmet; layers folded back upon each other, revealing a face underneath that was even further startling. Its head was the shape of a pointed cone, it had banana yellow skin covered in bumpy brown warts, a large mouth that smiled sharpened teeth, and three dark purple eyes in the middle of its face, each blinking in unison shifting back and forth between Konstanze and Leon. Leon felt horrified; he had seen a lot in his life but nothing like this.

"I choose not to put the dog down, furthermore, unless you and your partner lower your weapons now I'm going to snap this creature's neck and throw it at you" the being spoke mercilessly in perfect German. Leon glanced toward Konstanze who lowered her weapon slowly; the creature shifted all three eyes to Leon who was so revolted he jolted his gun down below his hips.

"What do you want?" Konstanze asked as boldly as she could. Leon observed her trembling, this was the first time he had seen her frightened.

All of the eyes shifted back to Konstanze, "You will come with me peacefully" it replied. The creature gently stroked the back of the dogs head with each stubby hand. "You have been chosen for the tournament that will decide your planets fate, and will come with me whether you like it or not" it told them, smiling maliciously after the last words.

"And if I don't?" Konstanze asked. Leon looked at her bewildered, wondering how she could challenge the thing.

"I will kill this creature" the being responded coldly, focusing two of its eyes on Chaz who sat peacefully in its arms. "After I've killed it, I will kill your human companion." The creature shifted glances back Leon, who felt a bit of urine trickle down the side of his leg.

"Okay, put down the dog and I will come with you" Konstanze decisively informed the creature; it obeyed, instantly setting down Chaz without harm onto the ground. Chaz ran off in the opposite direction of Konstanze and Leon, his tail in between his legs.

Konstanze began to walk slowly toward the being.

"Don't do this Konstanze" Leon managed to call out "don't take her, take me instead." He began walking forward toward the creature, unknowing what compelled his feet to move and uncertain of why he wanted to risk his life for her. The creature shifted its top eye toward Leon seeming to squint.

"Leon, stay back." Konstanze begged, halting Leon in his tracks. He watched as she

118

approached the being, it put a hand out, and reluctantly she put her hand towards it. Like a puff of smoke, they both vanished without a trace when their hands touched. Leon fell over, passing out.

Everyone in the Washington meeting listened intensely to every detail as the German Chancellor shared what happened to Konstanze. 47, seated across the Chancellor, felt compelled to mention as she rubbed her chin, "So, another one of these creatures spoke our language."

"You've been awfully quiet this entire time Prime Minister" the Ethiopian president sat back, observing his counterpart from the United Kingdom.

"Much like in Berlin, there was a nonviolent incident that occurred at the London Chest Hospital" Prime Minister Landon responded and gave a not so secretive nod for Agent to take the

floor on his behalf.

Chapter 7: Cardiologist Kidnapped

"According to all reports received from British Secret Service, a creature appeared in the hospital and took this one" Agent began to educate the other members of the room as 47 laid out a picture of a young female wearing her medical uniform, "This is Doctor Helen Hazell, age twenty six. She is brilliance in a generation where the average IQ's are dropping. She was studying at Oxford Medicine several years before most kids graduated grade school. With all of the opportunities she had, she chose to be a cardiologist so she could save lives. She's truly one of a kind."

"And the creature that took her?" Ethiopian President Asfaw interrupted.

Skellet pulled up another image on the computer. "Hospital security cameras picked up the image of the creature in one of the primary operating rooms. All reports confirmed that this one spoke perfect English. It gave a scare to one of the other doctors as well but he's fine" Skellet chimed adding on to the report.

Agent looked at the African man concerned, before delving into the story with the others.

London England, Europe

Saturday 06/06/16

5:00am

"Helen, you did not go home last night, we're all worried about you," Jermaine complained at the seat across from the woman who worked on an interminable stack of paper work at the desk. Jermaine was a very fit, handsome, African English doctor in his late forties; his unshaven face was proof he had been working just as hard as Helen was. Elaine, Helen's top aide, sat in the chair next to him fast asleep with an obstreperous snoring. Whenever Helen had an unpleasant evening, Elaine felt obligated to stay even if Helen ordered her to leave Elaine remained.

"It's improper you know. She thinks it mandatory someone needs to be here with you." Jermaine continued to preach at her before she finally looked up and responded.

"Do not continue to lecture me, Jermaine. The merger is about to take place and there is a lot of work to be done here" Helen insisted. She sat there with her large thick glasses drooping off her head as she wrote down a diagnostics of one of her patient's health. Helen was a pretty standard Brit looks wise in her own opinion; she was ten pounds overweight for her height and most viewed her as physically average, but that never diminished her intellect. Her heavy beige hair blended well with her snow-white skin, and the thick lenses of her glasses, hiding most of her natural beauty, distorted her oval brown eyes. She was voluptuous but her body was still youthful for being her age and working as hard as she did. She was the youngest Chief Administrator ever at the London Chest Hospital.

"Don't you pay people to do that for you Helen?" Jermaine questioned peering across the desk at the paper work. She glanced up at him and he retreated folding his arms across his chest. "You will learn some day, hopefully by the time you are my age, to slow down and enjoy some of your life" Jermaine spoke to himself at this point, he got up from the chair, and began to walk to the door. Before he could reach out and open it, someone burst through the other side slamming Jermaine in the face with the door. "What the bloody hell?" Jermaine asked flailing back and grabbing his nose. It was one of the new nurses working in Allergy Services, a woman dressed in light pink scrubs and breathing heavily, in her fifties easily.

"I'm so sorry, there is a problem and we need you now Doctor Hazell" the woman huffed taking a deep breath. Before Jermaine could turn back to Helen, the woman was up from her desk and throwing on her white coat.

"Helen, I can handle this," Jermaine told her, but she was already ahead of him, out the door and following the nurse.

The three of them cruised down the hallway to allergy services, though Jermaine was in much better shape than Helen he always had a hard time keeping up with her when she got to moving fast. "Right here, examination room number nine" the nurse informed them and Helen darted in with Jermaine in pursuit.

Upon arrival, they saw a man lying on the table, his face, and neck so swollen and red that he was barely recognizable as human. An elderly foreign woman yelled frantically in a tongue Jermaine didn't recognize and a young male nurse stood there trying to make sense of her frantic words. "Seafood allergy" Jermaine blurted out as the man on the table wiggled grasping at his throat begging for air.

"No!" The elderly woman responded back snappily walking to Jermaine and pointing her finger at him threateningly.

Helen walked over to the man to get a closer look, hives swelled on his skin along his neck and face. "Bee sting?" Helen asked the woman calmly in another tongue.

126

"Yes, yes!" The woman replied grabbing Helen frantically by the arm and guiding her to her husband.

"You speak Greek?" Jermaine asked Helen.

"Yes, but that was Albanian" Helen replied, she turned to the nurse smoothly, "Prepare me a shot of epinephrine and get this man an oxygen mask," Helen ordered the nurse who moved briskly. Jermaine nodded at the male nurse who scurried leaving the room. Helen turned to the woman and patted her on the head, "He will be okay mam; I'll take care of him." Helen took the prepared syringe from the nurse as the elderly Albanian man on the table had stopped thrashing as the nurse administered the oxygen mask. His face and neck had turned a shade of blue that began fading back to normal as oxygen reached his lungs. Jermaine watched as, without hesitation, Helen jammed the needle into the half-dead man's chest. His tiny Greek wife put a hand to her mouth in shock but the woman kept her composure.

"Well that got intense for a minute didn't it?" Jermaine commented as he and Helen left the room.

"Chief Administrator" the nurse, Kathy, who had retrieved them, called out from behind before they could make their way down the hall. The woman walked up to them as they turned around, "Thank you, you really are the best" she complimented Helen.

"No problem Kathy, keep doing acceptable work here and if you need me, you know where to find me" Helen responded giving the other woman a wink.

"Wow." Kathy replied in awe of the young woman, "You're such a professional. I can't believe you remembered my name" she applauded blushing and looking away.

"I never forget names. Everyone who works here is important to us" Helen replied spinning around. Jermaine watched Kathy admiring Helen for a second as she walked away, and he turned to follow the young doctor; this is why she was the head of the hospital.

"Helen, Helen!" Elaine cut them off in the hall; the young woman was still in her scrubs that she was sleeping in earlier, "Where have you been? They need you in cardiology it's an emergency."

Helen and Jermaine followed Elaine picking up the pace again until they reached the cardiology wing. Room 21 was a one of the fancier, brand new operating stations, where they exclusively took patients that were suffering myocardial infarctions or other serious heart issues. Elaine had no credentials for entry but Helen and Jermaine, both entered immediately, and the door sealed shut behind them. They observed the patient on the operating table surrounded by three other worried doctors, and hurried over to the sink and preparation station at the other side of the room. They washed their hands and put on surgical gloves. Elaine had said it was unlike anything she had ever heard about and the fact that three of the hospitals finest were here meant nothing was good. They walked over to the operating table, to the motionless body and the three other doctors who looked down. Nothing could prepare them for what they were about to see.

Jermaine peeked over Helen's shoulder, as he always did. As she stepped up to the body, she wedged in closer and he stepped closer as well, until he could finally see what Elaine had been talking about in the hallway. "Some type of metallic object is trapped in his chest" one of the doctors pointed to the open cavity. Doctor Ackerman was the senior cardiologist in the room and a man who knew his craft well. Helen and Jermaine peered inside; a shiny silver ball only a few millimeters in circumference had attached itself just outside the heart.

"What is it?" Helen asked and each one of them in the room gave her a blank look.

"His vitals are steady now; when he came in he was complaining of severe chest pain, he collapsed. His blood pressure was 220/170, his body began failing" Doctor Ackerman informed them with a solemn grimace.

"So we opted for open heart surgery to clear out what we thought was a problem with the coronary artery, when we put him under his vitals stabilized. When we pried open his chest this is what we found," an Indian veteran female nurse Cindy told them, pointing down at the object in the patients opened chest. Jermaine stared at the metal ball; it shined even while dotted and smeared with the man's blood. It was unlike anything he had ever seen before in his life and it seemed to be growing just under the left pulmonary artery.

"We don't know what it is, but it seems to have attached itself there, when we tried to remove it, it grew" the third, a short, bald Irish doctor continued explaining. A doctor Jermaine didn't recognize.

"Well, we have to remove it now, how much longer do we have?" Helen asked looking at each of them individually, "If it's killing him, whatever it is has to be removed" she finished.

"Helen if it's an organism or electronic, and reacted to touch by growing, we must be very delicate" Jermaine added. Doctor Ackerman took one of his tools, and very bluntly poked the metal object, the patient's body jerked and his mouth shot open very ghastly. Jermaine felt himself jump back at least a meter.

"Helen Hazell" the man lying on the operating table removed his oxygen mask and sat up looking at her; his eyes frosted over with a clear resin.

"What on Earth!" Jermaine shrieked in horror, but the other staff in the room looked unpassed. Helen took a step back on hearing this man in a drug-induced coma call her name.

"We don't know Helen" the nurse cackled spinning her head three quarters around to look at them, her eyes were also covered with the resin and she spoke in a profoundly wicked voice, "Every time we touch that object this man says your name."

"What is going on here?" Jermaine asked loudly in confusion as he walked backwards towards the door. He didn't know if Helen had kept her composure out of sheer exhaustion or if the woman truly had nerves of steel.

"Touch it Helen" Doctor Ackerman barked, white as a ghost and his eyes also covered in the resin.

"Helen don't do it; let's get out of here, this isn't right!" Jermaine yelled at her; the room went quiet and instantaneously the three staff members turned to look at him,

"You are no longer needed here, you can leave or die" the third doctor informed him. Helen turned to look at Jermaine and he realized it was too late; her eyes covered in the same resin. She reached into the man's chest with her extended grip as she had thousands of times before. Jermaine

134

made it to the door but as his hand pressed against the handle, he couldn't help but look back to see what was happening. They all watched her as she moved forward accepting a metal instrument from Doctor Ackerman and with the most precise movement, the metal tips connected with the shiny metal ball. This time the man didn't react at all. Jermaine let out a sigh of relief.

"It's unstitching itself from the artery," Helen stated confused, observing while the metal ball seemed to release the vital piece of the man's heart, "What on Earth?" Jermaine heard her cry out. She carelessly reached in with her free hand and lifted it up out of the man's chest; it was a perfect spherical ball, smooth as ice and speckled in red blood.

"Eat it" the nurse, insisted in her hoarse voice.

135

Jermaine and the others watched her as she brought the object close to her lips. "Don't eat that Helen have you gone mad?" Jermaine yelled; as he did, a creepy presence in the room overcame him and he fell to the ground, defecating in his pants. The patient from the operating table had sat up and reaching out he grabbed Helen by the back of the head with one hand, and shoving the metal ball into her mouth with the other. Doctor Ackerman shrieked out in laughter and the dead man on the operating table fell back.

"What in God's name! I have got to get out of here," Jermaine groaned as he attempted to stand but discovered he was frozen; all he could do was watch in terror, hoping it would end.

"What's going on in here?" he heard Elaine's voice behind him followed by a scream; the poor nurse passed out behind him. Jermaine was fighting

136

to keep his eyes open, something in the room was putting him to sleep.

"You'll be coming with us now Helen Hazell" the third doctor snarled; in the blink of an eye the three medical personnel in the room vanished being replaced by an identical silver metal sphere, each dropped to the ground. Hitting the ground they bounced once into the air before shattering into several more. Twenty metal balls the size of a quarter bounced back up into the air. Jermaine didn't understand what was happening as he watched them multiplied repetitively.

"What is going on?" Jermaine asked under his breath while managing to get on his feet. The spheres multiplied and bounced until they covered the entire opposite side of the room.

"It's not human technology" Helen replied complacently looking back at him again, her eyes

137

appeared coated with the clear goopy material. "I've never seen anything like this in my entire life," she said to him, slowly turning her head to look back at the marvel on the floor. As if reacting to her words, the spheres began to roll to a central location on the floor; melting together, they began forming into a solid mass.

"He he he he he" the being laughed as it took on its final form. What had started as one metal ball just minutes ago now became some type of silver robotic creature covered in a metallic armor molded with different patterns and symbols.

Jermaine pinching his arm thought surely he was hallucinating, perhaps he was unconscious on the floor somewhere, and this was all a dream. Helen and the creature stood there just looking at each other. "Helen we must run!" Jermaine somehow managed to yell out.

138

"Jermaine you should go home to your family" Helen's voice echoed out trembling.

The metal creature spoke in perfect a childlike English female voice that came from the helm through a barred screen around its mouth. "Congratulations Helen Hazell. You will represent your planet in the Tournament of Worlds. We will see you shortly."

Again, Jermaine yelled, "We need to run Helen, come on get it together" yet he knew he couldn't run no matter how hard he tried, he was so terrified his hands and legs shook.

"I wouldn't run if I were you unless you wish to suffer the same fate as him" a different voice, much older, and colder sounding, came from the helmet as the being pointed to the man on the table. A loud hissing noise, followed by a startling pop, thundered out from the creatures head. Like the sunroof on a car, the front of its helmet slid back and folded itself upward, revealing a nose less, one-eyed, and small-mouthed, wrinkled green face with yellow teeth.

"Are you an alien?" Helen, seemingly sedated, was able to ask bluntly. It was unlike anything Jermaine had ever seen in his life; Helen was right, there wasn't any possibility that it could be human. Jermaine felt dizzy just before crashing to the floor almost losing full consciousness, but being too worried for Helen he fought and was able to keep one eye open.

"I am Ordonimo" the creature introduced itself with a terrible smile; its yellow teeth had a blackness growing on them that gave the creature a rotten appearance. Its leathery green skin wobbled as Ordonimo encircled putting a clawed hand around Helen's shoulder, "As you say I am an alien; or you are, dependent on whose perspective."

"What, do you want with Helen?" Jermaine mumbled out bravely.

"I am shocked that human can still speak" Ordonimo declared to Helen looking over at Jermaine. Helen didn't respond or react in anyway.

"You will come with me" Ordonimo repeated, "That is my mission and so it shall be done" it finished. Jermaine could only see the back of Helen's head, but he knew she was trying to fight off whatever the creature had done to her; that's whom Helen was. "You will not?" Ordonimo answered for her, "Oka Oka Oka" the alien creature laughed strangely, its lips curled back giving it a menacing look. "You have no choice," it snapped. "My theatrical entrance into your world should have been enough to prove I have the power to take you at any time, but if you make me show you more, your human companion will die" Ordonimo pointed its clawed hand at Jermaine. Jermaine's first reaction was to try to stand and run. His legs began wobbling from under him as he reached out for the door handle. Suddenly Jermaine felt something wrap around his waist, looking down he realized he had been lassoed by something silver. He felt his body pulled back by a strong force, much too strong to overcome. Jermaine crashed down to the ground again falling backwards near Helens feet.

"Stop" Helen yelled at the alien, "I'll go" Helen told it nodding her head. Helen stood straight up and looked in the alien Ordonimo's one eye. "Do not hurt him," she commanded in an assertive tone. Jermaine struggled to his knees panting as he listened.

"Then come with me, and accept your destiny, Helen Hazell." Ordonimo as a gesture extended his hand out to her.

Hearing this story of yet another occurrence of these alien abductions the leaders in the secret meeting room looked at the images seeing the similarity and differences to the other aliens. This latest one was clad in the same silvery metallic armor though shaped uniquely with different symbols. Unlike the others, it had a completely revealed wrinkly green face, with short pointed boney spikes protruding into the air and abbreviated, pointed ears that stood up like a rodents. "So this is the real deal, this is the alien invasion that the films are made about?" President Feng grabbed his brow and looked down at the table in disarray.

"Subconsciously we as humans always knew a day would come when we may have to actually deal with extra-terrestrials, and we've all found the independent evidences they have visited us," American President Henderson interjected with pep, "Agent is the best of the best at what he does. Therefore, what we need to be doing is continue finding out the information that we have and proceeding from there. There's no time for discouragement Feng."

Vibrating sounds came from the table, each leader reached into their pocket to grab their mobile device.

"It's me," referring to her phone the petite Australian leader continued briefing everyone; "My team is here and they have an eyewitness. They're on the way down now." Her smile was uplifting for all of them since each story had seemed to spiral

144

into a stranger place. It was possibly the first time anyone in the room smiled; it was but for a moment as they all returned to the situation at hand, putting on a serious faces. The slice of exciting news did give a much needed calming moment.

Chapter 8:

Tournament of the Worlds

There was a knock at the door and in walked a very out of place Queensland police officer, wearing a crisp light blue shirt and shorts along with a darker blue police cap. Behind the Officer walked a young man that couldn't be over twenty years of age and wore a grey sweatshirt, blue jeans and sandals, he rubbed the back of his dirty blond scraggly hair as he looked at each of them before continuing. Behind him walked a young woman, possibly in her early thirties, she wore a suit just like the agents in the meeting. She darted ahead of the men to meet with Agent, bending down and whispering something in his ear. By the tired expressions on all of their faces, they had flown in straight from Australia.

147

"Officer you are free to go relax in the lounge, thank you for your duty" Agent informed the man standing and shaking his hand. The police officer looked around at each of them suspiciously then fixated his sites at his leader Lady Klem who gave him a nod of approval.

"Alright but this one here has a pretty sticky story. When he came to us we gave him a drug test, he was lit up good" the officer responded in Pidgin looking at the young man who had followed him in.

"We'll take it from here" Skellet replied in a dry tone, the officer glared intensely at him before turning and exiting the room.

"Everyone this is code name Sydney she is an asset from our allies at the Australian Secret Intelligence Service. She will be involved with everything from here on out" Agent introduced the petite woman, who shook each of the other agent's

148

hands. "Alright son, sit down and tell us what you know. Why don't we start with your name?" Agent questioned, pulling out the only empty chair at the table and dragging it along the floor to the newcomer.

"Hello everyone, I'm Chris" Chris spoke out meekly; he was nervous and had every right to be, "Chris Williams."

"Alright Chris, it's very important you tell us everything you saw, don't leave out any details" 47 attempted to calm the young man down placing a hand on his shoulder.

"Alright, but you ladies and gents won't believe me" Chris remarked looking up at each of them, "Is that the Queen?" he blurted out in shock looking at Chancellor Nimitz who glared at him with disdain.

"Oh lord, what is this?" President Golov asked staring at Chris, "Did you see an alien attack someone or not?" the Russian shouted sternly jolting Chris to the back of his chair.

After a moments silence Chris found his voice "Wait, you mean Hamlet?" he asked the Russian leader.

"Wait, what do you mean Hamlet?" Skellet asked.

"Yeah, I mean we met an alien dude, but he didn't attack us at all. He was the kindest dude we've ever met; David and I partied with that big blue fella before they had to go save Australia and everything" Chris explained to everyone in the room.

"This idiot is fried" President Henderson commented shaking her head; Landon chuckled.

"Maybe you should listen to his story, he had quite the experience" Sydney defused the direction of the conversation before someone else could put a barb in the obvious stoner.

"Yeah mate, maybe you should let me speak up I didn't do anything wrong" Chris chimed in looking over at the American leader who turned a shade of red.

"Well technically you killed an endangered species and ate it; you're in trouble if you don't tell them everything you remember," Sydney corrected him. Chris immediately began sharing his experience from the beginning.

"David is my Father's, brother's son, my cousin, and lifelong friend. He's Australian and Indonesian, his mother is a super intelligent Indonesian scientist. You could say this about David; the apple didn't fall far from the tree."

Gold Coast, Australia

Saturday 06/06/16

2:00pm

"C'mon mate down this way" David called behind him as he led the way down the narrow path, holding his surfboard above his head with one arm and carrying his backpack with the other, he led Chris through the deserted rocky pass.

"David mate, everything I've heard about this place is choppy, choppy, choppy," Chris hollered back. The two finally reached a small desolate beach, something that was rare in Gold Coast. All the beaches here were packed and if they weren't, it was due to the bad currents or the shark season. Chris knew David was an expert on Marine life though so there wouldn't be any sharks where they snuck off to surf. David was also a genius, born with a photographic memory, as well as a brain Chris never understood. David took underwater photographs of the many creatures off Gold Coast for a living; the high definition photographs of sharks, turtles and other aquatic life were immaculate pictures, but he never made any money doing it.

David replied while looking out at the water, "Today is the day and it may just be a special day." David was two years older than Chris was, twenty-two, but they looked the same age. They both had natural long scraggly hair that reached down around their ears in the popular shag cut; that was pretty much all the similarity between them. Chris wasn't naturally muscular like David who had very angular chiseled facial features, deep brown eyes and tanned skin like his mother, and a dark five o'clock shadow

153

just like his father. Chris on the other hand, had a pointy nose and blue eyes that looked as though they were squeezed together, along with several zits on his hairless cheeks that were an instant turn off to most women.

"What are you staring at bro?" David asked as he looked over at Chris picking up his board from the sandy beach.

"Those waves won't sit around and wait for us," Chris pointed out at the ocean. David's eyes followed Chris hand pointing at the beautiful rips that were forming on the top of the water. The two raced out splashing as they went just as they did when they were children; soon they were hitting the first wave that was sublime height. "Good call coming out here!" Chris yelled out to David as they paddled to the deeper waters.

"I told you mate, I came here the other day and spent the entire afternoon" David replied as they bounced over another wave. The two were up again, riding the next rogue wave in unison. Though David had brilliance Chris could keep up with him on the water, it was something they had done together since they were children.

"And I mean this wave was a gnarly one mates, we were like right next to each other..." Chris explained to the room. President Golov stared unblinking at the young man with a finger digging into his own cheek.

"Damn it" President Henderson snapped at the young man's seemingly insignificant storytelling, before the Russian lost his mind and attempted to strangle the dumb boy at the other end of the table.

"What? I'm getting there, hold on" Chris replied peeking around at Golov who ignored eye contact.

"How about one more wave and we go in and eat lunch?" David asked Chris as they paddled out slower than they had with the previous waves.

"I'm amped let's do it" Chris blabbered in the water as he sped ahead.

"Alright, almost there" David announced to Chris as they bobbed up and down over another ankle buster. The waves were forming just right and if they timed it correctly, it would be a freak wave just before lunch.

Chris went to yell back to David, but he never got the opportunity because he swallowed a mouth full of saltwater. They had 30 seconds before the wave came; Chris looked off to the side to spit out the water when he saw something out of the corner of his eye streaking through the water. A giant grey dorsal fin about 100 yards away began closing in on him and his cousin fast. "Oh no, look out a shark!" Chris screamed out to his cousin.

David heard his warning and paddling ahead of Chris he yelled back, "Here comes the wave, hurry up we can outrun it." The two paddled faster and the massive wave approached them; it was easily the biggest they had attempted all month. Chris felt himself freeze only for a moment before hopping onto his board and turning in the direction of the wave. He glanced over at David who was up, then looked in the direction of the shark. The dorsal fin was heading straight for them. The wave behind them began to tumble forward and Chris felt the surfboard propel him forward like a rocket. David took the lead, heading straight toward the dorsal fin.

"You're going to get bit idiot!" Chris

screamed again but it was of no use; the dorsal fin

appeared lunging straight toward them. Chris tried

closing his eyes but not in time to see, it wasn't a

shark at all. Something large and metallic popped

up out of the water and flew past them both,

crashing hard into the wave directly behind them.

Chris looked ahead at David who was starring wide-

eyed at whatever it was they just saw. When Chris

went to turn back, he saw, just for a second, the

large metallic being surfing the wave next to him.

It frightened him so badly that he felt himself lose

control, slip off the surfboard, and he slammed head

first into the water under the waves. Chris swam

through the water toward the shoreline where he

could see the creature and David in a standoff,

speaking to each other on the beach.

David turned toward him and called out "Come on up; it's okay." Chris unattached his surfboard tether from his ankle and jogged up to the two of them wearily. "Chris, this is Hamlet" David introduced the massive creature they had mistaken for a shark. Hamlet easily stood nine feet tall and had to weigh over 300 pounds. Chris couldn't see any of the creature's skin below the head and its humanoid body had covering of a polished plated metallic armor that ran horizontal. The alien had blue skin and chubby bloated cheeks, with pebble sized white eyes that didn't blink and sunk deep into its head. It also had a very human like mouth and navy blue lips that stretched out from cheek to cheek. When it spoke, the white dull teeth similar to a horse were visible. Hamlet and Chris looked at each other for a moment that seemed considerably longer.

159

"Hello mate" Hamlet acquainted himself politely, mimicking a human wave with his four fingered alloyed hand.

"Hello Hamlet" Chris waved back awkwardly straining his eyes to look at David without moving his head. He saw David was looking at Hamlet in curiosity.

"So Hamlet, what is it you want again?" David asked plainly.

"You will have to go with me later, but for now I would really like to eat some food with you both, my treat. My species suffers from the burden of having a voracious appetite" Hamlet finished rubbing his hand in front of his stomach in a circular motion clearly expressing his hunger. David's own stomach growl, but he continued cautiously observing the alien unsatisfied with the answer.

"Well can you at least tell us where you're from or what you are?" David asked with his hands firmly crossed. Chris felt confused by the entire situation and just stood there looking back and forth between the two as the conversation went on.

"Will you eat with me if I catch us some food?" Hamlet responded turning its hulking body and looking out at the ocean.

"What do you mean like a fish?" David asked stepping up beside it, looking where Hamlet looked out at the waves.

"I love Seafood!" Chris managed; David turned and shot him a look of disapproval.

"Locked on," Hamlet murmured under his breath staring out at the water. Lifting a mighty hand up Hamlet palmed the water moving slowly and in the midpoint of its hand, a tiny magenta ball of energy appeared fluctuating in size by only a few centimeters every second. Humming began and grew intense as the magenta sphere took the shape of a pointed rod; with a forward thrusting motion Hamlet launched the spear forward and it whipped about cutting through the water like a bullet.

Chris jumped back but David kept his composure. Looking straight at the being he asked, "Well did you get it?" Hamlet looked back at David; as a reply, he reeled his massive metallic hand back toward his head and took one mighty step back. David and Chris both looked out at the water seeing the beam snap and wiggle through a wave, and meaty dusky colored fish seemed to melt into the wave before crashing back down into the water. "No you can't!" David protested to Hamlet putting his hands up.

"It is too late David, this animal is mine by right of the hunt, and I will consume its flesh with

162

you and your human companion. It will strengthen our bond," Hamlet argued returning David's stare.

David looked back to Chris with his eyebrows raised as Hamlet reeled in the robust fish. Chris couldn't really believe anymore what he was seeing as he realized it was a dolphin struggling in the wake with the spear punctured through its side. This all had to be a bad trip. Chris shook his head violently and took a second look but nothing changed. "David, can you tell me what's going on here? I'm having a hard time understanding mate. Do you see this thing?" Chris frantically spoke exhaling the words as he pointed at Hamlet, who looked back at him with a wide grin.

"Yes, I see it. His name is Hamlet and he plans on murdering an endangered snub nose dolphin and apparently we are going to eat it with him" David focused on the dolphin that was shallow

163

enough now for Hamlet to literally drag it through the sand as it splashed around. A dark trail of blood followed the dolphin as it tried to make one ultimate escape but failed.

"Okay, whatever then" Chris responded lighting up another smoke and watching the scene play out as he took each drag.

"You know Hamlet; you could have caught a different fish" David implied as they watched the alien grab the sea creature and smash it on the head with its metallic fist killing it instantly. Brain matter and residue leaked out from the dolphin's carcass as Hamlet picked it up and threw it over its enormous shoulder.

"Yes, but another fish wouldn't taste as satisfying as the Australian Snub Nose Dolphin" Hamlet replied as he apparently shot a blast of

164

energy from his hand at the beach creating a six foot gap. Hamlet swayed his head left to right,

"You will need firewood if you want to cook the dolphin," Chris blurted out at it.

"Stay quiet" David whispered hitting Chris on the shoulder.

"Yes, I've found some west of here; I'll fetch it" Hamlet retorted, aiming his hand at the hole and looking straight ahead at the rocky path the two surfers had traveled to get here.   From above the ravine, several small pieces of dead wood floated through the air toward them.

"What the hell? I am flipping out?" Chris let out. He noticed that several tiny butterflies made out of the same magenta energy Hamlet had pierced the dolphin with, carried the wood.

"You aren't flipping out Chris. The moment he extracted the particle spear from the dolphin he had turned it into those energy flies that are retrieving the firewood," David informed his cousin while reaching for drinks from his backpack. David tossed a cold one to Chris who fumbled with it but managed to clinch it before slipping to the ground.

Hamlet looked over at David with a raised brow and commented "Very astute observations human. Not the wording I would use, but you have very natural keen senses. I wouldn't expect anything less from a champion chosen to represent his planet," Hamlet commented. The miniature flies made of energy dropped the dead logs into the hollow pit. Before dissipating into thin air, three more of them approached through the sky carrying pointed tip wooden stakes. Hamlet put the dolphin down on the beach, raised a hand in the air, and brought it down sharply, chopping through the fishes head. Chris had to turn away but David watched as Hamlet ripped the spine out from the body of the fish in one clean thrust.

"Well, I guess when one is offered elusive, almost extinct dolphin, you eat it" Chris remarked as the bonfire cackled from some fat dripped off the fish at the end of the stake he was holding. Hamlet and David sat in silence across from each other as the meat cooked.

"You could have respected what I said Hamlet. These dolphins are on the brink of extinction in this world" David breaking the silence attempted to lecture the alien, who pulled his dolphin out from the fire and took a generous bite. It stared intently at David while chewing the rubbery meat.

"It is a wonderful dish David, prepared by a fantastic chef. The chances are beyond comprehension it will be the last meal you have on your planet. I would eat it if I were you." Hamlet

replied, continuing by taking another super-sized

bite.

Chris decided to take a bite of the fish, much

to David's dissatisfaction. It was the best thing he

had ever tasted; it was rich and savory like steak,

but was juicy and tender like pork. It was obvious

Chris was smiling from ear to ear because David

chimed in as Chris chewed it quickly and

swallowed. "Is it really that tasty mate?" Chris

nodded his head before taking another bite. The

three of them were soon all eating the dolphin in

unison and sharing cold drinks. Hamlet laughed

loudly identical to a human as he chugged a beer for

the first time, much to Chris and David's

satisfaction.

"Well, that was delicious" David

commented, looking at the bare stake that had

served as a massive fork. Chris peeked over at what remained of the dolphin, not much, just the spine, head, and some bones tossed into a pile.

"I would not lie to you David; I'm ready to tell you what I can about the trials ahead for you" Hamlet suggested sipped another beer before letting out a light hiccup.

"Okay let her rip" David answered. Chris noticed his cousin had rapidly drunk five beers throughout the meal. David never drank like that in his life.

"When I arrived here on Earth today, I snapped an Xhorni particle that temporarily puts a halt to all time within the vicinity about the size of this beach. Have either of you noticed that the sun hasn't changed position from behind that cloud, though we've been out here for over one earth hour?" Hamlet asked looking up in the sky at the

169

beaming sun hidden behind a large fluffy white cloud looking like a plump sheep.

"We got some decent cloud cover today right?" David looked over at Chris who shot his cousin a fake smile. Chris didn't know how to respond, after all Hamlet just said he stopped time. Instead, David resorted to looking up at the sky at the same large cloud the alien was looking at.

"Enough about cloud cover. We don't have much time" Hamlet snapped his large metallic fingers together gaining their attention. "After the Xhorni particles energy is depleted, I'll take you to Platform. There is where you will make the transition from human citizen of earth, to one of the ten Champions chosen to represent your race in this cruel tournament," the alien explained.

"Okay, back up here" Chris finally interjected in the conversation with a passion, "How about we start with, who exactly are you?"

"I am Nulayatamashilon of the planet Odsistergbru VI. I've selected the name Hamlet because that's the actual translation in your language. I hail from a planet several light years distance from the major galactic highway that connects all of the galaxies together. In your language it is known as Orion" Hamlet responded to Chris's questions.

"Okay, Hamlet. So what exactly is your mission?" Chris asked feeling a boost of confidence based on the painless answer he'd just received.

"I'm here because I'm a slave that lives on Platform. Out of the thousand enslaved species, from all of the hundreds of known worlds in the Federation. I was chosen a second time, out of sheer

171

luck, to retrieve one of your planets contestants. To come to Earth and detain you David" Hamlet finished as he roasted another piece of the dolphins flank.

"You are a slave?" David asked, lighting up a joint with his hands, "You don't wear slaves armor, and your weaponry isn't that of a slave," David questioned. Though the alien was massive enough to handle Chris and David as it pleased, it had instead been courteous and very thoughtful.

"I'm a slave of the Galactic Federation of Trade, Hospitality Entertainment and War; one of two of the most powerful entities in the known galaxy. They equipped me with this armor and a weapon named in your language as a Spiritual Enhancement System. In exchange, I serve one of the leaders on Platform obediently, or obedient to an extent at least" Hamlet responded with a chuckle.

172

"Well why are you a slave? Why don't you just run away from this Federation thing?" Chris asked while Hamlet demolished more stake.

"The Federation came to my planet much like they are coming to yours now. It was the second anniversary of the ancient tournament for my home world. Nevertheless, we lost, our people were enslaved or exterminated; our cultures destroyed; life was eradicated. What is left of my people live in a small colony in the mega city; located on the Federations mothership Platform, Arhgripye."

"What?" David questioned, "What do you mean your people were enslaved?"

"In the Tournament, the masters will dictate whether the region of your planet that you represent is worthy based upon a single combatant's survival in three rounds of dueling to the death. First the planets champions are chosen, then the first round duels are set up" Hamlet continued almost losing both men in the conversation as he spoke rather quickly.

"So are you a past champion? Did you have to compete in this tournament?" Chris blurted out asking the alien.

"I'm not a champion. I was a simple cook on my planet when Platform arrived in the atmosphere. I come from an advanced race, much like the human species except we valued life; we were very gentle and our numbers were limited. War hadn't existed on our world for a very long time and by the time the Federation arrived the warrior class was extinct. The ten champions chosen were extraordinary beings, the very finest of our race. There was only one chosen from my planet that made it to the final round of the Tournament. There she lost her life and our planet lost the tournament. The masters combed over our world with Platforms ultimate weapon the Lapatrin, destroying most of our infrastructure in one day. Seventeen millions of my people lost their life in a matter of moments. Just before they drove us to extinction, they sent a massive army of their personally trained forces called Bylar to enslave us. I've heard rumors that they're still in the process of turning it into a luxury resort for the richest of the races" Hamlet finished and both of the Australian men sat in silence. Chris thought deeply about all of it and the whole situation made him dizzy.

"That's awful" Chris let out looking over to David.

"Why are you telling me all of this? Why not just follow orders and take me to your ship?" David asked Hamlet, who gave him a toothy smile.

"Because you bear a huge responsibility, David Williams. I've studied you and all of human kind on Earth, after I received my orders to detain you to fight. You are a modest and intelligent being. You must find your inner strength or the same thing will happen to your planct that happcncd to minc" Hamlet explained.

"I understand" David calmly replied.

"What? What do you mean you understand?" Chris asked his cousin, "This is an alien from another planet that wants to take you away so you can go die on some space ship for people who have never done a thing for you."

"Don't be so selfish. It is an honor to be a champion chosen from your world," Hamlet spouted out, giving Chris an awful glare.

"It will be okay. I'll make it through cousin," David replied looking at Chris. A fat tear welled up

176

in Chris's eye as he sat there looking at his cousin with admiration. David had said that same expression for years, diving with sharks, surfing in storms, roughing it in the outback, and he always made it through. Chris nodded his head at his role model in understanding.

"You will be equipped with state of the art weaponry" Hamlet added, "Everyone on Arhgripye is talking about the warlike humans of Earth" Hamlet gawked trying to lighten the mood.

"Well, I was fortunate enough to have an intelligent captor, who probably smuggled a Xhorni particle down here so he could give me a heads up about all of the stuff that is about to go down. Can you tell me anything else about why I was chosen or selected?" David asked. Hamlet was flattered but not surprised David had remembered such information passed on to him.

177

"As I said, ten of you were chosen on Earth based upon a certain median of attributes far beyond any other beings that inhabit your planet. The attributes the scanners notice in other beings aren't only physical, but mental and especially spiritual. Each of those chosen possesses top .01% in each category and usually has a specialized profession that others in the world cannot do" Hamlet explained, Chris and David both understood everything this time and they nodded following along.

"So you're like super Aussie" Chris smiled, trying to gain a laugh. David didn't respond so Chris followed up the remark by asking Hamlet, "Can you tell us anything about the tournament that will help him live?"

"Yes, but after this David and I must go. We have run out of time. Chris you can go to your local

178

authorities and tell them what you saw here today. When you get to the leader of your nation, tell them not to attack Platform, whatever they do. Ra is the over aggressive leader of the entire Federation, he will contact Earths leaders when the Champions have all been collected. Remember, they must not attack Platform, no matter what," both David and Chris agreed to the terms, so Hamlet could continue. "After the champions were collected on my planet, Platform loomed over our most important city, Wewjiel. The Federation broadcasted the tournament daily as entertainment in every home. During that time, they landed ships on our world and introduced new goods. They make millions in credit off our people while introducing new technologies, virtually enslaving most of the population before we had the opportunity to wise up. The high class from my race took opportunities

179

to get off our world and go to resort worlds. I've found out since they were all enslaved and sold into cheap labor on various industrial planets. Every day was a battle fight in the massive arena located on Platform in the heart of the city. One million beings from around the galaxy fill the seats and cheering on the competitors. While Ra and some of the richest beings in the galaxy profit on each battle from their private suites. The fighting in the Tournament is three rounds total" Hamlet finally stopped. Chris tried his best to absorb everything he had just heard as the alien caught its breath.

"Wow three rounds, three duels" Chris murmured under his breath.

"Yes three rounds" Hamlet started up again, "They will announce your opponents after all humans have been collected. Each round you will face a harder adversary. Round one, you will fight a tier one slave chosen at random from the galaxy, similar to me. Round two, you will fight a trained soldier known as Bylar and have full control of their SES. Round three, you will fight a veteran warrior hand selected by the people of the galaxy" David took a deep breath in, but Hamlet wasn't finished.

"After our Champions were taken, it took one human week for the spiritual enhancement systems to fully adapt with their bodies and to train in the Realm of Rol. Humans rate as a mediocre race though they have a natural affinity for war. Your race is in the middle tier because of your feeble body structures and unpredictable emotions, yet are high spirituality and adaptable" A beeping noise came from inside Hamlet's suit of armor that finally cut him off; he looked intently over at David.

David turned to square up with Chris. "Well, I love you cousin, tell everybody I love them," grasping him in a bear hug, it was goodbye sadly.

"I love you too mate" Chris cried, the tears visibly rolling down his face onto his cousins shoulder.

David spun back around to face the alien; "Well let's go then Nulayatamashilon" David genuinely surprised Hamlet this time as he remembered the full name. Hamlet reached out a hand to the young man; David extending his own hand back they both disappeared in the magenta colored energy.

Chris sat back in the chair, wiping his face of the tears that came out. The entire room of leaders seemed captivated by the story and there was such a deep silence a pin dropping would have given one of them a heart attack.

"There are two more, note it down" Agent broke the silence, directing 47 who jotted it down on her mobile device. Agent turned around pulling out his own mobile device, "we need an escort for a young man heading straight to decontamination, he has made direct contact" Agent gave another order and slid his cell phone quickly into his pocket.

"Decontamination, Agent?" the Australian Prime Minister spoke out against such action, but Agent ignored the woman. Lady Klem turned to Sydney who looked away from her. The door opened and Chris was escorted from the room, Sydney following close behind.

"Thank you son, you did a good job" Agent thanked Chris just as he exited the room.

"We needed that" Skellet let out a sigh after the door finally shut.

183

"Bet your ass we needed that, it was a lot of information" Agent responded. The room was silent as they could all see the gears spinning and turning in each other's heads.

"We will prepare a top weapons arsenal coordinated and approved by the leaders in this room before the spaceship that's called Platform arrives. When Ra arrives on our planet, we will not attack them as advised, but will listen to their demands and gain more information as to what this Tournament of the Worlds is," Agent informed each of them plopping back into his chair.

"What if the aliens show aggression? Surely, we have learned they are not all friendly like this Hamlet. I saw one myself that had no interest in surfing, smoking, drinking, or eating dolphin" President Golov rebutted Agent as expected.

"As far as we know President Golov, your alien could have just been an unintelligent slave having had no concept of communication; much like a gorilla on our planet. We must understand realistically there are many species out there in the known galaxy, and not all of them will have a grasp on superior communication skills," 47 answered the Russian just before the Ethiopian President Asfaw fired another question from across the table.

"If we are to stand a chance against an alien invasion, we must all share arms equally. The African Union is no military nation like Russia or the United States" the darkest leader in the room attempted to gain aide as he looked around at the many white faces.

"I don't think discussing arms distribution should be on our list of priorities Mr. President. It is unlikely that Ethiopia will be any alien invasions first or primary target" Skellet rebuked his own leader pointing out facts.

"I think the best thing for all of us will be to go home, get some much needed rest and to expect communication from this Ra in the next few days. We can contact each other via video chat and discuss all further specific details in closed meetings like this," President Henderson stated sitting firmly with her fingers intertwined together on the desk.

"I would love to get back so I can report everything we've found here today to the royal family. They've been throwing a tantrum," Prime Minister Landon agreed standing up and gathering his belongings.

"I wouldn't mind being back on Russian soil either. These secret American buildings have never been a favored meeting location of mine...reminds me of a rat den" President Golov chimed in slyly.

"I can't wait to get away from your stubborn ass Golov. You make everything difficult with your abrasiveness" the Mexican President mumbled to no one in particular, Golov looked at him but chose to ignore the opinion.

The other leaders looked at each other and slowly nodded in approval, each stating their final piece while standing up from their chairs. The numbers in the room began to diminish until only President Henderson and Agent stood there together.

"Agent, well done leaving out the complete conversation the alien had with Helen and Max. Does Prime Minister Landon know?" President Henderson asked after congratulating him on his secret knowledge.

"Not yet. We buried it with two M16" Agent answered pondering about the alien that kidnapped Helen who had remained the screen, "If they had known all of the information, there would be an imminent scramble for positioning within the Federation and it would mean immediate war" Agent spoke to the President casually.

"Your new job, as of now will be to garnish a position for me within the Federation as soon as Ra arrives. Make sure it happens before Golov can make a move, I want my family safe and on board that ship as soon as possible."

"I understand" Agent responded with a raised brow of his own.

Chapter 9: Into the Realm of Rol

Hamlet stood behind the medical examiners, observing the contestants from Earth, each human seemed to be in superb condition. They floated naked in the thick purple Elyx gel as the weaponry system fused with their bodies. Above the tanks on a rectangular monitor each of the humans, fantasies were unraveling.

He walked up closer and read each nameplate that was encoded in basic tongue. Bai Lo from the Asianic Chinese race dreamt of being locked away in a lambent orange uniform, in a tiny concrete room with metallic bars. Hamlet watched as Bai shook trying to wake, but when any being entered that purple liquid chamber there was no awakening until death or until the spiritual enhancement system was fully fused. Hamlet stepped forward to the next enclosure, a blonde

haired female human named Lucya Konstantinov,

the Russian woman ran away from her own

shadows. She ran faster, and continued running

unable to gain any advantage on the shadow man no

matter how long or hard she sprinted. Hamlet could

not read the blank expression on her face, knowing

that it must be a dream the scrawny human had

constantly. Hamlet reached Maximus, the

American; in Arhgripye, everyone had gone wild at

the selection of the half-black half-white American.

Most people were placing their wagers on the

warlike culture that region had produced. Hamlet

glanced up at Max's screen. He was in bed with two

luscious female humans that had opposite hues of

hair, and a green paper with human faces on each

side rained down from the ceiling. Hamlet smiled at

the primitive male human before continuing. Next,

190

the female Konstanze Nimitz dreamt of a fair sized, multi colored, hairy earthen beast. They played together on a dark green patch of earth with a circular object that floated through the air. The woman would throw it and the beast would collect it before the round device hit the earth. Catalina Cavaco of the South American region, another popular culture among the substantial betters, dreamt of a man taking her forcefully in the bedroom. Hamlet observed as a couple of the examiners chuckled at the humans lust filled dream, but Hamlet showed no interest in the human mating ritual and moved on. Abdul Khaleel of the Arabian region was next in line, the human looked wild compared to the others, his black beard reached down to his chest, and very eerily his eyes remained open as if he was looking outside at them. On his monitor he was running through a building searching for something, the dream was so frantic and rapid it was hard to focus on anything and Hamlet moved on unwilling to see what it was the man would find. Tesfa and Aishwarya seemed to share the same dream. The dark skinned African male dreamt of several little children playing around him gleefully, it was clear in the vision he was their protector. The young brown skinned female next to him, Aishwarya Kapoor, dreamt of two miniature children resembling her genetic DNA, as they followed her on a trail in an environment of plants with brown bark that shot up to the sky blocking out light from above. Hamlet nearly reached the end of the line when he came up on a fascinating dream. Helen Hazell, a female who wasn't as physically together as the other females, but was deemed the most intelligent among the entire group. She had her hands deep inside another

192

human's chest. Hamlet watched with curiosity but moved on to the last container. His human friend David floated there peacefully, in the dream he was having, he was swimming through the water taking pictures of the marine life. Hamlet smirked thinking how casually his human target had handled the entire event that took place on earth that brought him here.

Hamlet walked away, this would probably be the last time he would see the contestants in person until the first round was over. He looked back one last time glancing at David's chamber and said the words aloud, "Best of luck to you little human. You will need strength in your heart to make it through this."

Platform Space Shuttle-Location Unknown

Sunday 06/07/15

Time: Unknown

Max tried opening his eyes, but the air felt too sharp, the light seemed to spike into his pupils causing a burning sensation when he tried opening them. How did he get here? How much time had passed? Everything felt wrong. He felt his mouth open and the glob of purple liquid gurgled upward from his lungs. It all came out at once as Max lay there sideways unable to control his body as it contorted. The spectacular sensation wasn't leaving as he kept shaking and the thick purple liquid splashed out of his mouth onto the dirt as he tried to inhale. When it was all out, Max opened his eyes and gasped for air, trying to put his hand out in front of him. His body was stiffer than wood, he was paralyzed neck down.

Damn it, Max thought as he blinked while his vision continued to phase in and out of focus.

194

He could feel the purple liquid secreting from his nostrils and running down the lower left side of his jaw. Move your hand, Max kept thinking, trying to focus on any type of change in his body besides his eyes. "Argh" Max was able to call out as he frivolously worked to put his hand out by his head. He wiggled enough that his arm fell from the side of his body where it had been perched. Max blinked again as he looked down at his arm.

"What the hell is this?" Max cried out looking down at the hundreds of blue vein sized wires that ran vertically down his arm and led to his hand, extending all the way do to the fingertips. They weaved in and out of the surface. His brain began to go further into panic mode but as it did, his finger twitched. "Progress" Max growled looking down at the hand.

"Just don't tell me you made me a cripple waist down Lord and I'll thank you forever" Max coherently blurted out. He felt a rush of blood go to his head and spun his neck enough to look up at the sky, it wasn't blue, black, or even grey laced with clouds, but a hazy tangcrinc color mixed with bright pink and a blinding white sun. Max had never seen a sky of that sort and it was almost as startling to him as the hand.

More time passed before he finally was propped up on his hands and knees. Looking around he observed his settings. Max was in a clearing surrounded by massive trees with forest green bark forming a canopy of pastel pink and royal blue leaves, and revealing only the circular space of the sky he had looked up at earlier. A woman, a real beauty, lay naked just as he was, ten yards from him on the lime green colored grass. As he looked at her

196

she began going through the same violent sickening process he had went through, puking up the liquid onto the ground without control. She had bleached blonde hair reaching her shoulders and pale skin that made her hourglass figure seem like she was a Barbie doll taking a dirt nap.

"I see you over there, and I swear to God when I'm fully functional you have some questions to answer" Max rumbled out while looking down at his hands. The wires were literally embedded in the skin; the heftiest of them ran down each of his fingers.

Max kept tapping each of those fingers as if playing the piano, as he watched the woman begin to move just as he had. She began by twitching her feet first, something Max had tried without success. As he watched, the woman began to move her feet faster and faster; Max got a strong feeling of envy as he kept tapping the fingers trying to regain control.

"Hey I don't know what the hell you've done to us or where we are, but don't you dare think for a second you're going to get up before I do" Max yelled out at her. The woman spun her head as if possessed turning around to look at him. She had freckles covering her high cheekbones, a button nose, and she gave Max a piercing stare with her green eyes. Max quickly tried to give one solid attempt at standing up but his feet gave out and he fell forward on his face. Most of his muscles tightened and tensed as he tried to move again, so he remained with his face implanted in the dirt. Max began counting the seconds as he tried to twitch his feet back to life. Seconds turned into minutes before Max finally felt himself gain the strength to stand, he looked to where the woman had been laying, but she was gone.

"Oh well, that's not good" Max mumbled out to the nothingness of the woods trying to gain full composure. It looked like he had gotten himself up north somehow, probably on bad drugs with that woman. Max held up his hand to his face looking at the wires that were surgically inside of him. With his other hand, he grabbed the thickest of the wires tugging it like a guitar string. An overwhelming burning sensation came over him pumping through his whole body; it brought him to his knees as he jerked in pain. Max hobbled back up to his feet in time to hear something coming at him from behind and fast; the woman. Just as she was about to hit he spun but couldn't muster the strength to lift his arms to defend himself. He felt the foreign branch she ripped off one of the nearby trees smash into his side and toppled towards the ground. Scrambling to his feet, he was able to leap forward dodging the next attack; he spun to face her, both arms falling limp at his side.

"I don't care who you are, You're going to answer some questions" Max challenged the woman who began backing up to the edge of the circular clearing, grabbing her breasts with one hand and covering her privates with the branch as she crept back. Max growled at her as he advanced forward in her direction, his body was coming back to strength.

"Who are you?" the woman asked him in an intense English voice, her eyes bugged out wide as she looked down covering her mouth with the hand that had covered her breasts. She looked across at him and noticed he was checking her out as a wolf does sheep. She rifled her hand back down to cover her chest again.

200

"I'm the one that's going to ask questions here. That night in the club, you said a bunch of confusing stuff about a tournament, and some Ra character. I didn't understand a damn thing you said, so how about we skip to the real questions. What is this stuff some type of tribal tattoo?" Max panted, exposing the discomfort as he ran a finger down one of the lines in his arm.

"I don't know what you're talking about, how would I know any of this?" The woman replied fiercely taking another step back, this time dropping the branch causing her to grab her mouth with both hands. She had made it to the edge of the clearing and inched herself closer to the forest as Max followed. Glancing back at the trees Max noticed how broad each one was, the bark on each were covered in a forest green moss. His mystery woman made a sudden move, jumping behind the nearest tree, hiding herself completely from him. Max hesitated about ten feet away and could only hear her words come from behind the tree, "I don't usually speak English unless I want to, something is happening with my voice I can't speak Russian," she informed him. "What is that supposed to mean?"

Max replied using his strength to jump around the other side of the tree with his hands up ready to fight. She greeted him with a solid front kick to the chest that knocked him back and nearly off his feet. Max recovered coughing up a fragment of the sticky lavender snot onto the ground; he brushed off the blow to his body, standing up. The woman was peeking at him from the other side of the tree curiously. Max was never one to be shy about nudity. He knew he was muscular and well endowed for a man; he took in her stare standing his ground firmly. "Should I be scared? Are you trying to make it fall off with your eyes?" Max asked the woman half-jokingly; she snapped her head the other way in embarrassment, her cheeks turning a rosy pink making her freckles vanish. Max couldn't fathom who she was, but his snide comment didn't stop her from turning and looking at him again. "You aren't the one who did this to us are you? And you certainly aren't the one who was at the nightclub that night" he conceded, "What is your name?" he questioned before she could say anything.

"Lucya" She responded meekly expecting him to exchange names formally.

"So, Lucya, any idea how we got here?" Max asked the woman who seemed to be opening up but this woman on the other side of the tree remained silent. "Well, I guess we are in a similar

203

boat. Naked out in the woods without a clue where we are" Max stated mockingly. He tried to peer through the woods for any sign of humanity.

Lucya came out from behind the tree. As she did, Max noticed black clouds of gas began dropping out like balloons from her fingertips. The woman shrieked out in fright as these bubbles seemed to float with her body as she thrashed out with her hand to try to stop it. The pint-sized gas bubbles automatically made their way to her privates and breasts, covering the exposed areas. Max was in awe, both at the extraordinary occurrence that was happening on Lucya's body, and how truly gorgeous her eyes were. The woman's face was naturally refined, just like a princess. They locked eyes as she attempted to calm herself. By the time he reached her side, the gas had evaporated; in its place were black spandex boy shorts that hugged the woman's rear tightly; and a white spaghetti top that concealed her once naked breasts. Max must have been staring, as she looked down at the ground giggling, "Maybe you should try the same thing" she suggested.

"I don't know how you did that but none of this is natural; maybe I'm dreaming" Max replied turning his body away from her. He rubbed his head in remembrance of what had just happened. Suddenly a jolting sensation was coming from his hands and he felt his body twitching, ten royal blue electric sparks escaped, one from each fingertip. They all occurred at the same time bouncing up and down his body until reaching his chest, legs and feet. It startled Max; but he felt the clothing as it formed around him, a crisp fitting white tee shirt and a pair of grey sweat pants, along with a new pair of white on white Nike sports shoes. "So, I think we need to figure out what the hell these are," Max suggested holding up his arm to show Lucya, who also had similar engraved appendage. The wires ran identical through both of their arms, and ended at their fingertips. Max began looking Lucya over, observing a black bead the circumference of a penny that jutted out from the side of her throat, "What is that?" Max asked pointing to the tiny abnormality.

"I don't know. I felt it earlier. It feels like there's a fruit stuck in my throat" Lucya responded poking the contraption with her finger.

"Maybe that's why you're speaking English" Max observed.

Lucya frowned looking back at him, "You really don't remember being abducted do you?" she asked. As she finished the words, both of them heard something approaching from a distance. It almost sounded like an airplane, but as it advanced nearer it wasn't a mechanical noise, it was someone yelling as they flew through the air. Max turned his attention to the pitch as it screamed out, and he spotted a black speck in the oddly colored sky that got larger rapidly.

"Arrrrrrrrrrrrrrrrroooooooooooooooooowwwwww wwwwwwwwwwwwwwwwwhaaaaaaaaa" a creature, Max could see it soaring awkwardly through the orange sky, as it came crashing down to them landing on the opposite side of the clearing. It spun out bunglingly but remained on its feet and ended in dramatic fashion standing upright, it faced Max and Lucya with four arms crossed across its body.

Max remained vigilant, expecting to see the woman with the assault rifle that had been in his club. Instead, what he saw was the extreme opposite, a gaunt alien with ashen colored leathery skin, standing the same height as Max. It had two fatty lumps jutting out from the top of its circular baldhead, with round pure black eyes that didn't blink as it looked back at them. The only clothing it wore was a beige robe that covered the mid abdominal region to the feet, and on each of the four wrists was a golden colored ring. Looking at Max and Lucya with an awkward smile revealing shiny silver teeth, it waved at them as if it was an introduction.

"Hello there humans" it said with a perky but slightly garbled male voice, "I'm Serta, your guide in the Realm of Rol" Serta introduced itself as it limped forward with a jerky gait. Neither Max nor Lucya replied as they watched the creature walk, both seemed to be in disbelief of what was directly in front of them. Max blinked his eyes shut; when he opened them back up, he expected to find something different, maybe his bedroom ceiling or the bottom of a table at the bar. Max noticed Lucya take a defensive position putting her hands up and taking a step back with one foot as if ready to run. Though he was inclined to do the same, he didn't.

"Oh, you don't want to start confrontation with me, though I understand your initial reaction. System calls for only two responses; I promise doing either will not work so just hear me out" Serta revealed stopping in his tracks. Then the alien put all four of his hands up to the sky as a means of surrender.

"If it came down to a fist fight between you and me pal I'm going to knock your head off" Max suggested pointing, but the alien chuckled at him putting one of the hands to its mouth.

"What are you?" Lucya asked the newcomer, lowering her guard before Max could challenge the creature and extending her arm over to Max, trying to sway him from being aggressive.

"My name is Serta, I'm one of five guides and a former champion in the tournament you have been chosen to fight in" Serta explained, wobbling closer to the pair. Max put his hands up again, but Serta was next to him instantly, a fraction of a second hadn't passed when the alien stood directly in front of him. The alien grabbed both Max hands with all four of his and pulled him in close staring at the human with the black unblinking eyes. Max was trying to pull away but something held him in place, a feeling of dread that started in his gut and flooded over his body. This powerful presence held him there paralyzing his mind. Serta could kill him at any moment if he pleased. Max wanted to scream out in agony, scream out for help, for anything, but he couldn't move.

210

"I see you've already activated your spiritual enhancement systems to cloth yourselves," Serta observed, releasing Max's arm and hobbling over to Lucya. Serta grabbed her arm and Max watched as both of her eyes went black. Lucya was in the same trance that Serta had just placed Max in, "Yes; yes, very comical, humorous indeed. Believe it or not you're advanced for such a primitive race," Serta stammered along, releasing Lucya from the grasp.

"Why is it I'm thinking Russian but speaking English?" Lucya asked the creature, as it waddled forward before turning to face them.

"All contestants, guides, trainers, the announcers, even Shu and Ra have had a Xanoraminix Metrophilier implanted in their neck that will translate all wording to the most common yet profitable foreign tongue on the host planet. Earths chosen language this tournament was

English" Serta answered the question casually then turned his neck pointing at his own tiny black device attached on the outside of his skin like Lucya.

Before Max could correct the creature, Lucya did with less aggression, "Isn't the most popular language on earth mandarin?" Lucya asked.

Max looked Lucya up and down for a moment, pondering what the woman did for a living.

"Very astute human, but that's a question I cannot answer right now" Serta responded turning his back to them, "You will both have to come with me. We have a ways to travel before we reach the others; you may ask me other questions on the way."

"What's the point of asking you questions if you're just going to dodge the answers? You're trying to avoid her question, but I'm sure you realize a lot of this doesn't make sense to us. Quit being a worm and give us straight answers" Max was getting agitated. The man was clearly not eager to take orders from the alien.

Serta wrenched his neck back to look at Max, the aliens circular eyes slanted as he scowled at Max. "Have you just insulted me human?" Serta asked. As he did, the sky around them began darkening; a gust of wind blew and howled against the tree line cutting at Max's face. Both Max and Lucya looked at Serta through the wind as the alien's expressions became animated.

"Stop" Max yelled across at the alien, Serta was reveling in the anarchy of the moment. Trees crackled, and the whipping wind spun blue and pink leaves violently to the ground. Lucya was pushed back by the sheer pressure the creature exuberated

213

from its body but Max grabbed her by the arm, keeping a firm grip.

"Please stop this, we don't know what we did wrong" Lucya yelled, pleading with the alien, The wind ceased suddenly, the trees stopped shaking and the sky returned to normal almost as fast as it had happened. Max and Lucya both regained their composure as they looked across at Serta.

"What was that power?" Max asked to Lucya under his breath, keeping his eyes focused on the alien.

"Be careful what you say this time idiot" Lucya scolded Max shooting him a look of disapproval.

"As one of five guides in the Realm of Rol, I reserve my right to kill any champion that disobeys or offends me" Serta wiped his hands together as he explained to the two, "However, I've never killed a past champion and I don't plan on doing so today, so if you could just follow me we can talk further."

Lucya reacted instantaneously, marching forward as Serta turned around and began heading the direction that he had flown down from in the air. Max hesitated but Lucya turned and motioned him forward so he trotted to the opposite side of alien.

"Serta, what exactly is this tournament?" Lucya asked as they were led into the thicket of the green jungle.

"Great question Lucya Konstantinov" Serta replied looking forward with a gloomy expression as they walked, "The tournament is a celebration of life, death, and everything that happens in between" Max gave the alien another irritated expression but Lucya shot a warning glance upon reading his face.

For now, he needed to remain quiet and listen. They quickly reached a path of golden chunky grass cutting through the trees into the unknown. Before Lucya could ask another question, Serta continued explaining, "A duel between two beings of tremendous capabilities, almost infinite potential; a duel to the death." Serta looked over at Lucya, "Is that the answer you're searching for human?"

Lucya nodded gulping down his words, but Max could no longer hold his tongue and asked in rapid fashion, "What do you mean? So there is a chance we're going to die here?"

"Yes Maximus Smith" Serta replied continuing, "There's a chance that all of you will die here."

Max stopped looking at the back of the creatures head as they walked, unknowing what to say at first, but then the words came to him. Max puffed out his chest, took one reinforced step forward, and spoke out, "I'm not going to die here." Serta laughed, spinning around abruptly. Lucya took a step away from them both, looking with a sense of urgency. Max also stopped, checking the creatures disposition, expecting anything at this point. The fact that he had been selected for this insanity was ludicrous enough but that he had to deal with an unpredictable being was numbing. For now, all he could do is follow, so he stepped on, walking right past the alien and down the snake like path.

"Great, that is wonderful news human" Serta turned back around slowly, staying even with Max's shoulder as they walked. Lucya trailed this time, unwilling to risk the scrawny alien's wrath. "The Tournament consists of three duels per individual" Serta continued, "You will be tested mentally and physically. but most of all spiritually, as you hone yourself into a living weapon." Ahead Max could finally see a clearing where the woods ended. Bright light illuminated the trail they followed showing the brilliantly orange color of the sky in the Realm of Rol.

"So we will be forced to fight?" Lucya asked in more of an aggressive tone than Max had expected. Looking over at her now, Max could see the strain on her face as she bore a hole into the back of Serta's bumpy head. The creature didn't respond; they already had their answer.

Max rubbed his eyes once in disbelief as they finally reached the clearing; it was as if he had stepped back into the time of dinosaurs. The view they had was impeccable scenery that revealed they were walking on top of a mountain; in front of them was an amazing ravine that went as far as the eye

218

could see. Vegetation with a Cerulean tint sprung up from the canyon forming an ocean like canopy. Max blinked as the entire site he was taking in dumbfounded him.

"The Realm of Rol training grounds to every participant in the tournament since the final war between the Federation and the Homon" Serta explained pointing at the skyline as Lucya and Max both marveled. To Max's right a cocoa colored path cut through the trees leading to a raging waterfall, taller than any he had seen; it was launching thousands of gallons of electric yellow liquid into a river disappearing into the trees. As Max focused on the magnificent site he could hear the running waterfall's thunderous noise as it poured over the edge.

"What is that?" Lucya inquired in a reticent voice, pointing left. Max took his eyes off the

219

alarming substitution for water just in time to see a humongous humanoid creature with oddly shaped pointed wings, soaring through the air above the tree line. It soared downward spreading apart the canopy-like display as it vanished without a trace.

"That was Lazzca, another of the guides here in the realm," Serta explained, looking over at the waterfall. Max blinked again with disbelief, everything was so incredible it caused dizziness as his mind raced about to take it all in.

"Why me?" Max blurted loudly. Lucya seemed to be wondering the same thing.

"You have both been chosen to represent your entire species, it is the highest honor one could ever hope to receive" Serta replied dryly. Max concluded somehow the aliens answers would always fall short of what he expected. Serta went on leaving no time for thought, "Come, we have a quite journey before we reach Alter."

Serta began walking down the trail that led towards the waterfall. Max and Lucya dragged behind. "This can't be anything good" Max stated to his Russian companion, who only raised a frustrated brow and began jogging to follow the alien.

"Serta, what if we win the tournament?" Max asked catching up to the two as they walked down the dark brown dirt path. Max began imaging the kind of prizes a powerful alien species might have in store for them if they won. Lucya looked over at him again giving her frown of disapproval; Max got used to those looks and didn't entertain her by exchanging glances.

"Your life, your planet, and the most powerful weapon ever created throughout the known galaxies, the SES." Serta was quick to respond, and although the answer was disappointing to say the least, it gave Max the impression that the creature's personality and desires were much different from his own.

"The Spiritual Enhancement System" Lucya pondered, raising her hand up again and poking the veiny like device on her fingertip while they walked, "What is it exactly?" she inquired.

"You will learn soon enough little human," Serta exclaimed. "In the pre-rankings released in Arhgripye, you were ranked as number one Maximus Smith. Lucya you were ranked number four" Serta informed them, "I'm thrilled that I get to watch both of your progress this next week."

"Ha" Max couldn't help but force a scoff, "What is this, fantasy football? Truth is, I love to fight so naturally I'd be number one" Max confessed to the alien bringing a thumb to his chest, as they strode together in unison. Serta began letting out a garbled noise that sounded like he was releasing a massive amount of air underwater. Max was sure the alien was laughing and for the first time since Max had gotten into this mess, he began to feel confident. Lucya opted to walk meekly behind them.

"Truth is, all ten of you love to fight you just don't know it yet" Serta replied, laughing again. Max caught on and forced himself to chuckle with the creature as they continued in the direction of the waterfall. Continuing along Lucya trailed behind and seemed to fade away from Max's mind.

Time passed as they traveled in silence, but Lucya broke that silence raising the next question. "Serta, is there anything else you can tell us about this tournament?"

223

"Let's see, you will fight the first round against a slave, most likely selected from Arhgripye or one of the resort worlds," Serta answered in more of a perky tone than it had been before. Max looked over at the creature subtly. Their guide didn't seem this warm at first. "In the second round, you will face a trained warrior, probably someone stationed here on Platform. If you make it past the second round, you will have the opportunity to face a past champion of the tournament. Only the most able and supreme beings make it through an entire tournament, it will be a true test for each of you."

Max rubbed his chin while they walked, snapping back into thoughts about the seriousness of his situation.

"Almost there" Serta looked ahead down the path with his charcoal eyes. Max could see the glittering silver teeth again, a smile, and hear the

224

humongous waterfall as they approached, "The Lanyrint, one of the five lifeblood's that feed the Realm of Rol" Serta finished as they rounded a corner, the noise of the falls was so deafening Max couldn't clearly make out the last words. Max and Lucya looked at each other as they saw the bright yellow liquid flow rapidly and descend hundreds of feet downward into a river that looked like orange juice.

Serta turned to Max first and gave him an awkward grin before appearing at his side as he had earlier, "In we go!" Serta yelled out as Max felt the alien grab his arm. Doing his best to keep his footing and pull away, he realized he couldn't out muscle the slender alien. Max was lifted off the ground into the air, his body propelled forward by the massive amount of force the creature extruded from its hands. He spun through the air looking

back at Lucya as he flew directly over the waterfall
and feeling the air escape his lungs, descended
down plunging into the ravine while wondering if
contact with the liquid would kill him. When he
reached it, he desperately tried to wriggle his body
straight. The impact went smoother than
anticipated; Max was able to put his feet down and
expectedly glided through the yellow ooze like an
arrow. Deep into the abyss he dropped, until he
finally lost momentum, regaining control of his
body. Snapping back up from the liquid, he felt
Lucya drop like a bullet into it next to him.

Chapter 10: Down the River of Myx

Helen felt herself slice through the liquid as she made impact with the yellow river thrown into by their guide Edna. First, the African, Tesfa, was tossed with little effort and now her. Yellow splashed around her as she tried to propel upwards but the gravity caused her to sink further. As she finally got control, something grabbed her. A digit wrapped around her ankle shaped like a rope squeezed tight, pulling her away from the safety of the surface. She let out a giant gasp of air and looked to where the tentacle led; she discovered a giant crustaceous creature surely dragging her to doom.

Helen began to run out of breath but saved became enveloped suddenly by a golden colored sphere of light, out illuminating even the color of the yellow water. Helen could barely breathe as she

227

open her eyes to see herself pulled by this highly

illuminating light encasing her body like a bubble

from the Kraken. She looked over just in time to see

Tesfa swimming on top of the sphere guiding it to

the surface. The African man, who had been

incredibly cordial with her, swam without

movement cutting through the liquid as he pushed it

away from his body with this shell of the golden

light that protected her. Reaching the top of the

river all of her senses returned as she heard the roar

of the waterfall and Helen feebly reached the murk

covered dark grey shoreline coughing up some of

the liquid she had almost swallowed gasping for

more air.

"Impressive, well-handled Tesfa Wolde"

Edna mumbled to them as they crawled up to the

shoreline. The compact, pudgy, pure mustard

skinned alien guide who wore no clothing stood

above Helen. Helen turned her head as Tesfa stood up beside her. The mystical energy he had created to protect them ceased, dissipating into the air.

"I told you, we are going to make it through this together," Tesfa whispered to Helen, his white teeth glowing brightly behind the dark skin and soaking wet black tee shirt.

"Thank you," she weakly replied. When they awoke naked, she had an intense panic attack and accidently injured Tesfa with her spiritual enhancement device; in return he forgave her, clothed her, and reassured her. Edna had arrived explaining he would be escorting them to a meeting between all ten contestants, adding this process was normal for those selected.

"Why did you throw us down here?" Tesfa asked Edna, as he lifted Helen up by one arm helping her stand.

229

"It is all tradition" Edna replied. Clapping his hands together once with authority. The alien had made it perfectly clear when they first met that if he clapped his hands, it was a warning sign that it was the conclusion on any topic the humans had brought up.

Tesfa looked at the bulbous alien and released a breath, calming himself down before confrontation. Grabbing Helen by the shoulder he asked, "Are you okay?" She nodded her head in assurance.

"Now that we have arrived at the first level of the Realm, we can travel via the river to our designated meeting destination," Edna directed, catching the attention of both humans.

"What is it?" Helen asked looking at the waterfall as it crashed into the docile river below.

"It is called a Lanyrint, and it feeds this entire realm with the lifeblood Myx, it's the equivalent to your water" Edna attempted to explain.

"So the liquid is Myx, the Lanyrint is the waterfall that sustains this massive indoor environment." Helen noted Edna's surprised expression indicated she was spot on. Tesfa rubbed his hand on his head, checking their surroundings. The sky was a mix of fiery orange, red, and yellow hues. The trees were taller than the eye could fathom and ringed with tiny pink crystals that jagged out from the green and grey barks. Only things reminiscent of Earth was the ankle high green grass and brown dirt they had walked on to get to the waterfall.

"Doesn't feel like we're indoors," Tesfa argued without point, looking into the sky with his dark eyes.

"She is correct though." Edna confirmed Helens' intelligent conclusion as they began to walk down to the river's edge, "We are inside a training facility where for seven human days you will perfect your spiritual enhancement systems and become champions of your planet."

"The Spiritual Enhancement System?" Helen questioned as she held up her wrist and dainty hand observing the tiny wires that formed around her appendages flowing into her fingertips.

"We have to swim in that?" Tesfa asked Edna concerned, which interrupted Helen's thoughts. Edna turned around, the yellow beach ball sized stomach bounced as he did, before it fell again overlapping his unisex genital region. Helen

232

couldn't help but notice the alien's blank privates; when it first introduced itself, there was visibly a perfectly smooth area between its legs hinting his species reproduced differently.

"Some challengers do, but I would advise you come up with something different." Edna responded, holding his chunky three fingered hand out to Helen, "Helen, it is time for your first lesson." Tesfa and Helen looked at each other with hesitation before Helen stepped forward, accepting Edna's invitation. She slowly crept to his side and he turned back to the river. "Myx, the lifeblood from the liquid planet Rizen V" Edna began explaining the liquid crashing rapidly into the jungle. "Just like water on earth, throughout the planets of the Federation this liquid sustains life and is used for multiple purposes, from medications to vaccinations, to advanced weaponizations," the

233

alien continued. Tesfa made his way to the other side of Edna, who waved the two hands in a circle conjuring two vials out of thin air. Helen noticed, unlike Tesfa and herself, Edna, a past champion, had complete control of his own capabilities.

"What will the reaction be if we drink it?" Helen pondered aloud, accepting the vial from Edna's yellow palm.

"Not for humans. I will guide you, Helen." Edna swayed his hand gently toward her, "In the galaxy, all living creatures large or small, stupid or brilliant, have one thing in common. We all have a spirit or soul"

"A spirit?" Helen questioned curiously.

"A spirit. It is the power inside of everything and everyone keeping every living creature at task. It gives us purpose; it guides all of us through life and helps form who we are as unique

234

beings. On your planet, humans often confuse spirit with instinct, heart, passion, religion, or power. These are all simple misconceptions of a much greater inner power that rests in every being in the entire universe, which is far vaster than the human species could imagine" Edna explained.

"Are you trying to say there is no god?" Tesfa asked aggressively, bluntly, and getting caught up with the religion aspect of what the alien had just told them.

"No, but I understand how you would ask that, being in the situation you're in now" Edna responded just as assertively. Helen took a step back expecting the booming clap of the creature's hands due to Tesfa's strict religious conviction, which showed sharply on his face but it never came. Tesfa finally let out a disobedient huff, deciding to stick with his beliefs. "For your own sake, Tesfa, your belief in God is a belief held on many planets besides earth. It will dominate your SES and may make you the most powerful contestant here, so you must hold onto who you are throughout this tournament. You must continue to believe" Edna explained to the man who looked at the alien with uncertainty.

"We are expected to create a craft or way to transpire the surface using our SES. We will go down the river of Myx and be meeting at the next destination" Helen exclaimed changing the focus. She had figured out what the training exercise was and it caught both Tesfa and Edna off guard.

"Excellent Helen; the Myx will naturally infuse with your SES temporarily giving you an increase to your capabilities. The tricky part will be imagining how you will get from point A to point

B. If you can draw on the new powers unlocked within, the rest should come naturally."

"So wait. Where do we go?" Tesfa asked. Edna lifted his blubbery arm gently and pointed down the river.

"You will know when you reach our destination. It is all a journey from here young human" Edna answered and continued, "In this training exercise, I will attempt to better clarify how to draw out the SES's power more easily, though Tesfa you may not need any help. Please step back." Edna motioned his large hand, shooing them both away and up the shore. "Now I want you to both follow my lead." Edna informed them, holding both of his hands out towards the river." The large alien closed his eyes and seemed to focus entirely on drawing out his own SES's abilities. A grey mist quickly spewed forward from Edna's fingertips, forming into a small-customized craft that sat on top of the flowing Myx. The alien made a loud grunting noise and the outside of the grey vapor shelled off forming into a metallic platinum substance surrounding the craft. New amounts of metal mass splashed down into the water and began to float with the current of the river.

"Amazing" Tesfa acknowledged, looking mesmerized at the craft as it floated away from them, gaining rapid speed and disappearing deep into the forests lining the riverbanks.

"Yes well, I haven't conjured in sometime. Yours and Helens will probably not be the same, seeing you're still in the baby steps of learning" Edna answered Tesfa while looking at Helen who watched Tesfa as he bent down behind Edna and scooped up a full vial of the Myx. "When you drink the Myx, you will want to think of how you are going to transport yourself from here to there. Focus all of your thoughts on that one topic" Edna continued lecturing but as he did, Tesfa guzzled down the liquid. "Such an impatient race" Edna began with warning but it was too late. Tesfa's eyes glowed in the same golden yellow that had saved Helen from drowning. It seeped from the sides of his eyeballs and corners of his mouth like steam from a sewer.

"What is happening?" Helen asked, ducking behind Edna's tubby body.

"He didn't give himself any time to focus before drinking; the Myx will instantly infuse with your SES putting you into an uncontrollable state, his mind is fluctuating" Edna explained to the frightened woman. "Tesfa, now we will find out if you sink or swim. Hopefully your instincts are as superior as the scanners hoped," Edna started as it moved forward, grabbing Tesfa by both arms

tightly. "Here we go" Edna yelled and with one

massive motion, the alien threw Tesfa into the air,

higher than any human could throw another human.

"No!" Helen cried out, as she watched Tesfa

glide in slow motion through the air; as if reacting

to her words, the golden mist spewed out

uncontrollably from both of Tesfa's hands and

swarmed to his back. Tesfa was so high in the air;

he was half way up the waterfall they had come

down. Helen observed in terror as the man began

his descent; his body began tumbling lifelessly, the

effects of the Myx still taking place. Right before

the man's limp body was going to land in the water,

Helen closed her eyes, unable to watch the impact.

"Her, Her, Her!" Edna seemed to laugh

neurotically before yelling out a compliment,

"Wonderful Tesfa!" Helen opening her eyes looked

at Tesfa, the golden colored mist still exhaled from his mouth every time he breathed, but Tesfa's back had grown two massive, feathered, golden wings that resembled angel wings. "Now go!" Edna hollered pointing down the river. Tesfa turned looking at them before sprinting through the air; the wings carried him causing a wake in the water as he soared. "Incredible for day one" Edna admired as Tesfa disappeared into the trees, "Truly I thought he would be ranked the highest among humans having been the biggest murderer on your entire planet" Edna commented, the words caught Helen off-guard. She stood there, shocked, at a loss for words. "Don't be surprised, Helen. Every human you meet here, even you, has taken another humans life at some point," Edna told her, looking at her with concern. The alien was foreign in every way and unclothed, but it attempted to show some empathy.

241

Helen looked directly at the white oval shaped

pupils in the aliens eyes but didn't respond.

"Especially for you Helen; this experience will be a

taxing burden," Edna continued, "You are unique

among the competitors."

"I shouldn't be here; I never wanted this; I

never asked for any of this" Helen began; she could

feel her nerves start to give way.

"Helen, you will learn you belong here just

as much as everyone else." Edna replied, "Now

drink."

Helen had been standing there looking at the

yellow filled vial for at least five minutes; Edna

hadn't said a word to her but she could feel his eyes

on her. She knew what she had to drink the Myx;

she just couldn't find the courage. Finally, putting

everything else behind her, she downed the shot and

focused everything she could into getting to the next

destination. A bright white mist unlike Tesfa's or Edna's poured out of the palms of her hands, forming two solid lines, wrapping around her ankles and snuggling up against her bare feet.

"Yes, well done" she heard Edna as she tried to look down the river. She felt herself stepping out onto the flowing liquid.   Helen had attempted to conjure roller blades that would cause her to float above, half of it she got right as she continued to glide out to the middle of the Myx. She couldn't tell what it was around her feet, the uncontrollable power of the SES streamed out of her eyes, distorting her vision. "Now go! Go, Helen!" Helen could hear the final words Edna shouted in the background of her subconscious. She looked ahead down the river and into the forest, the next destination carved out in her mind. Helen crouched down and with one thrust of her right leg, she was skating on top of the water, flying down the river and spreading the yellow ooze on each side as she accelerated. Helen could feel the artificial air blowing through her hair; she kicked her legs, skating above the deep canyon of flowing Myx underneath her, it brought a cooling relief. For the first time since she had gotten into this predicament, Helen looked ahead through her blurry vision and smiled, kicking out another leg and thrusting forward at an inhuman pace.

Chapter 11: Earths Champions Meet

"Come on, you can do it. Let's pick up the speed" Konstanze tried to encourage Aishwarya. Since she had met the Indian woman, Konstanze had felt there was a large difference between the two of them. Aishwarya was beautiful and dainty; Konstanze was tough and gritty. Aishwarya must have only been in her mid-twenties; Konstanze looked young but was going on thirty. Aishwarya had slim dark brown legs that stretched out and gave her a couple inches on Konstanze, who was taller than most. Aishwarya had incredible jet-black hair and deep brown skin enhancing on her perfect frame that caused the white tank top and shorts conjured up with SES earlier, really stand out. Konstanze was the definition of a hard-nosed German woman. Although some considered her attractive, she prided herself on being rough and keen.

Aishwarya rowed much slower in the teal tinted wooden canoe than Konstanze's spiritual projection of her dog Chaz could run on this imitation of water. It seemed like hours earlier when their alien guide Pike told them to continue down the river. Konstanze could tell the effects of the Myx were wearing off, especially for Aishwarya who physically struggled to paddle. "I'm just feeling a little tired is all; maybe we should take a break?" Aishwarya suggested, as she barely dipped her row into the water. "I'm not a Police Officer like you Konstanze" Aishwarya whined.

Konstanze felt a pang of guilt. Aishwarya had explained she was a college professor at one of the Universities in all of India. She'd been cornered on the side of a mountain while on vacation in the

Himalayas. Based on what Pike had told them, Aishwarya was here most likely because of her super brains, not her super build. The skinny woman finally caught up to Konstanze and took a second to float next to the big brown spiritual dog that Konstanze had easily summoned after one a drop of the Myx.

"I know. I'm sorry Aishwarya, but we must be getting close to our destination and we have no idea where we are or if we are in danger. It's just best to move as quickly as we can" Konstanze attempted explain and persuade the woman into quickening her pace, to no avail. Though she had only spoken English for the first time a few hours ago, Konstanze enjoyed hearing the words fall from her mouth. It sounded classy, far different from her usual German, and it came effortlessly.

"I'm doing my best. If you want, you can go ahead of me. Did you ever think of that?" Aishwarya released her frustrations on Konstanze, who took it personally.

"You know what? I have thought of doing that, but I wanted to stay with you to make sure we both made it there safe" Konstanze spat out beginning to lose her own resolve in dealing with this foreign woman.

"Why don't you just go ahead then? Go, clearly you don't have the patience to wait around for me" Aishwarya huffed rowing the boat, putting her back into it and darting a few meters ahead of Konstanze. Konstanze took it as a challenge and her spirit canine raced with each paw floating just above the yellow Myx. She zipped past Aishwarya before the woman could say anything else, kicking up the liquid all over her recently dried hair.

248

Konstanze didn't look back, though she could still hear Aishwarya screaming out for her to slow down; she had gotten off on the wrong foot with the her from the start when they both woke naked after their arrival from earth. The alien guide Pike hadn't spoken much to either of them and only made matters worse when he had disciplined Aishwarya early, by zapping her with a bolt of energy from his finger when the other woman asked too many questions. It had put Aishwarya on her back and crying. The alien was a foot taller than any human Konstanze had ever met and crueler than any criminal she had detained. It had dark purple fur that lined its body and a face similar to that of a pig. Pike wore tight fitting camouflaged green and black metallic armor, and had two arms, hands, legs and feet like a human being.

249

Konstanze could no longer hear Aishwarya as she sprinted further down the river. The trees on each side of her were only a haze as her spirit animal howled loudly roaring forward meter after meter. The SES system had immediately produced the canine in the shape of Chaz when she drank the Myx. Konstanze held on tight to the sides of it imagining her real companion by her side. Something ahead sparkled in Konstanze's eyes and she could see a massive opening to a bay ahead where the river flowed out into a lake. Konstanze's spiritual energy barked out again as she lunged forward no longer concerned with Aishwarya. Konstanze finally reached the end of the river and straight ahead of her, a barren, flat island with baby blue blades of grass seemed to be calling out from the distant side of the bay. This was it; Konstanze could feel it was the destination point. She could

250

see little dots moving in the distance, other figures on the islands shore were already gathering. Swiftly she remembered Pike had said there were eight others besides herself and Aishwarya. Had other humans made it there before her? Konstanze's oak colored spirit beast ran furiously above the water with even more determination.

Konstanze reached the shore and she could see her guide Pike, along with four other aliens huddled together in a meeting. Two other humans on the shoreline stood together deep in conversation. As she approached the shore, Pike managed to divert his attention to her and walked down near the humans. "Well done Konstanze. You're the third to arrive" Pike bellowed out to her in his raspy voice.   She looked back in his reptilian eyes thinking how he'd been quiet rude, speaking only in riddles to her and Aishwarya. Now

251

he walked forward, past the two male humans and up to her seeming different. Konstanze's spirit canine dissipated as she jumped on shore, and she planted her feet on the grass that felt rubbery. Dizziness came over her as she tried to walk forward; her legs became wobbly and she almost fell down to the ground before someone grabbed her as she spun, falling backwards.

"Don't worry, I fell too," the man whispered to her, she felt his forceful arms lift her up. She stood taking him in; his youthful tanned unshaven face sculpted with a strong chin, thick messy hair, and hazel eyes giving him a look only the Americans had. He wore a crisp white t-shirt and grey sweat pants, unlike Konstanze, this man was able to get himself into some shoes.

"I'm Max" Max introduced himself to Konstanze in a kind tone. The man kept his arm wrapped around her waist "You're going to be okay, what's your name?" he asked her. She looked at him and pushed his arm away from her.   Pike had wandered back over to the other aliens and they spoke to each other in whispered voices about something urgent. An African man, wearing commando pants and a black t-shirt with dark skin and a balding head with frizzled hair walked up from behind them.

"I'm Tesfa. What is your name woman?" Tesfa assertively introduced himself asking the question again. This man stood shorter than Max but seemed stronger; by the many scars revealed, she concluded he was some kind of soldier.

"I'm Konstanz," she replied without pleasantries, staring out at where she had come from, hoping that Aishwarya would be okay. As she thought of her, all of them heard a screeching noise

253

coming from the distance; they each turned and could see a red-hot streaking light coming from a different corner of the lake.

"Bai" Konstanze heard a female voice come from the aliens. The most extraordinary of the four had yellow skin and didn't wear any clothing. It had bulbous facial features and chubby ears with earlobes that dipped down before curling at the bottom like a corkscrew. The beings smooth belly hung down covering his or her private area and it had fat legs that led down to two large feet with only had three bare toes.

The next alien, the one that had said the word Bai, was much more petite, built very humanoid and feminine. She had light brown colored fur covering her womanly shape and spiked up at the top of her head forming a wild haircut. She wore what looked like an assault squad uniform, carried a rifle on her back and had a bushy tail that extended down forming a diamond shape.

Konstanze watched as she began to walk to where the approaching light was coming from.

"Whooooooohooooooooo" Konstanze could hear the light yelling out from the distance.

"Who the hell is that?" Max asked the others, first looking at Konstanze, who returned a raised eyebrow shaking her head, as they stared out at the approaching light.

They could see Bai as he broke into the basin, the yellow Myx on both sides of him bursting outward before splashing back down into the lake. It was an Asian man and he was moving at incredible speed, running on top of the lake so fast a fiery substance of red followed leaving a path in his wake.

"Amateur" Max turned his gaze away from Bai unimpressed, walking towards the aliens, leaving Tesfa and Konstanze to watch as the outsider approached.

"Bai welcome! Nicely done, you've managed to place fourth" The female alien called out to the Asian man as he landed on the beach in a squatting position; his fiery trail disappearing just as his feet touched the ground.

"Fourth? What do you mean fourth?" Bai spat out as he gained his footing looking up at the other humans. Unlike Konstanze, this man seemed to walk fine as stood up and approached them. Unlike all of them, he was shirtless and wore only a pair of black sweat pants. He was muscular with ripped definition covered in visible scars and tattoos. Bai walked past the aliens, right up to Konstanze and Tesfa, his damp black hair and dark eyes fixated on her. He didn't stand as tall as they

did but Konstanze could feel his spiritual energy
was so dense.

"Hello woman, you're a pig aren't you? I can
smell it on you," Bai hissed at her, bowing his head
and giving her a fake smile.

"What did you just say?" Tesfa asked Bai,
moving forward to Konstanze's side.

"You heard what I said black man, you
going to do something about it?" Bai replied
standing tall and taking another step forward,
unimpressed with the display of intimidation Tesfa
was showing. Konstanze didn't pay attention to the
bickering and didn't care what Bai called her, as she
spotted another person arriving. A solid black
bubble shot across the water's surface noiselessly.

"Lucya is here Serta" Max announced with
relief, walking past Tesfa and Bai. The contestants
watched as she approached and Konstanze noticed

the alien with black eyes and grey skin, draped in a human like robe waddled over near them.

"I told you she would be fine," the alien mentioned to Max as it walked up behind him. He had bumps on his head the size of coconuts with grey skin and black almond shaped eyes. Max turned to it giving it a dirty look as it walked up next to him. The two began a quieter conversation as they got closer to the water's edge to greet the woman Lucya.

"So where do we go from here, Jazir?" Bai turned asking the female alien. The man walked over to Jazir, Pike and the yellow alien.

"Wait patiently and everything will be revealed human" Konstanze heard Jazir respond and they began their own conversation.

"Congratulations Lucya. You've managed to place fifth, far better than expected" Serta welcomed the woman as her bubble faded when she touched the shoreline. Konstanze watched as Max grabbed Lucya as she began to fall, just as he had grabbed her. Lucya was a beautiful, blonde-haired woman with toned legs and crystal like green eyes. Adorable freckles covered her face giving her a look of pure innocence as those eyes fluttered up at Max.

Soon another arrived and it seemed to excite the guides standing on the shore behind them as they all scurried down to where Konstanze and Tesfa still stood. A purple dorsal fin jutted out of the water, ripping apart the Myx with force.

"Wow, someone actually chose to swim" Max observed as he, Lucya, and Serta walked up.

"Hello, I'm Lucya." Lucya introduced herself to Konstanze as her and Max joined them.

259

"Konstanze," she replied looking at Lucya with cold eyes, unknowing if she would be fighting her fellow contestants or if this would be something completely different. At this phase, all she could do was be courteous. Lucya noticed her vibe and stood quietly, watching the lake as the next person approached.

"So who was the first to get here?" Lucya asked Max under hear breath but loud enough for Konstanze to overhear.

"Me. When we drank the Myx, something happened, I didn't mean to bail on you." Max told her crossing his arms as they all watched the purple fin come closer.

Out of the water, fifteen feet from shore popped up another man; he landed on the island a few meters from them. He was young and muscular very similar to Max but taller with longer shaggier hair. He didn't bare any battles scars like Bai or Tesfa and only wore a pair of swimming shorts. The Myx flowed off his body as hunched over catching his breath. "David?" One of the aliens next to Konstanze asked in a grizzled tone as the man landed on the shoreline in front of them. Konstanze looked to her left at the mustard colored alien. "So Abdul isn't here?" David asked them standing up straight his tight abs had crevices that formed a ripped pack. Konstanze's attention swayed from the yellow alien back to the new human. David stood even taller standing straight up, the man shook the remainder of the Myx out of his soaked hair.

"Did you really swim here?" Max asked David, gazing behind him out at the lake.

"I had no choice. Another competitor wouldn't stop attacking me" David scoffed walking past everyone before taking a seat on the blue grass.

261

"What do you mean?" Konstanze asked David who walked away from them.

"I mean from the time I woke up and saw the guy next to me, that lunatic was trying to kill me" David responded putting a finger in his ear and digging out more of the liquid, "You won't want to meet him. Even Lazzea had issues with nut job" David finished.

"So where is everybody from?" Max asked Konstanze.

"Germany, Berlin" Konstanze answered first, to get the basic question out of the way. She watched as everyone else felt obligated to acknowledge the question.

"Moscow" Lucya followed up so Konstanze didn't feel alone.

"Detroit, United States of America" Max answered himself, looking next at Bai, Tesfa and then David.

"Gold Coast, Australia" David answered, Konstanze looked over at him; he stayed reclusive, away from the group.

"Africa" Tesfa said secretively. The man seemed wary of answering any questions he wasn't asking.

The entire group changed its focus to Bai at once. Even the guides were intent on listening in on the human's conversation. "China" Bai said in a smug expression, whirling around and walking away so he didn't have to talk to the others.

Another light caught Konstanze's attention from the distance to the left. Was it Aishwarya? The other contestants looked over as it approached, racing across the water. It was unlike any of the other SES Konstanze had seen; another black light but this one was unlike Lucya's. As the object approached, Konstanze could draw a comparison to her own means of transportation. It was a woman with wild dark black hair riding on top of a creature with many legs; the oily blackness gave off an illumination that seemed to swallow any light around them. The creature skirted across the water until it drew closer and closer.

"Another one" Lucya said, pointing to the right.

Konstanze could see the other was a petite woman, younger than the rest of them. She skated through the air as she pressed her legs into each thrust gaining momentum. Konstanze searched the Myx Lake for any sign of Aishwarya.

"You said there was a contestant that attacked you?" Konstanze asked David, spinning

264

around on the beach and looking at the darker skinned Australian man that was relaxing in the shade.

"Yeah, his name was Abdul" David responded, sitting there with his arms on his legs scanning the new women that just arrived at the beach.

"What is it, Konstanze?" Lucya asked Konstanze, noticing an immediate change in demeanor from the German woman.

Konstanze turned around to Lucya, and over the Russian woman's shoulder saw Aishwarya paddling her tiny teal canoe into the bay. "No, it's nothing, never mind. I just got worried about the woman I woke up with" she informed Lucya. At that moment, after meeting all of the other humans, Konstanze wanted to run out and greet the young Indian woman. Compared to the others, Aishwarya may not be fit for a fight but she was truly a kindhearted person selected into the wrong situation.

As if reading Konstanze's thoughts, Serta interrupted the arrivals of Catalina and Helen, "We have trouble," the guide shouted loudly, looking into the distance to the left. "It's' Abdul he's coming in charged up, I can smell it" the alien informed his fellow guides. Konstanze looked back to where David had been, but he was no longer there.

"Incoming" Edna called out putting both his hands out to the sides before bellowing, "Humans stand behind me I will protect you."

Konstanze and the others were only able to take a couple of steps back before they could see the dark burnt colored sky become laced and then filled with a neon forest green color, like thousands of bolts released from crossbows, foot long green

266

streaks of spiritual energy glided towards their target, the island. As it got closer, Konstanze realized the entire area where they stood could end up demolished by the onslaught. Edna put both hands out toward the incoming mass, Serta, Pike and Jazir all stood boldly by the pudgy yellow aliens side.

"How could this day get any worse?" Max asked as the bolts began their steep descent towards them. They all watched in disarray, as the amount of green dots seemed to multiply as they magnified getting closer.

"It's him," Pike commented, looking back at the group, "the wild card from your planet, Abdul"

Right before the arrows were about to strike, Konstanze saw David disappear beneath the Myx out of the corner of her eye. Edna put both hands up toward the sky, and as each of the green arrows approached to thrash in and obliterated them all, they exploded at impact against an invisible shield Edna had erected using his personal SES. Each green substance slammed into the unseen wall making a booming thud that shook the ground beneath Konstanze's feet.

The alien, Jazir, pointed out at the lake at a green shadow of man seen walking on the Myx in the distance. The remainder of his white ragged clothing flowed in the wind as he began a sprint directly at them, green spiritual power flowed out of his eye sockets and his mouth; behind him the darts of the fresh energy were forming and launching themselves into the sky at them.

"Damn human must have over juiced on Myx" Serta coughed as they stared ahead. Max stepped forward and Serta turned back to them sharply, "Stay back, we have it handled" the alien warned them.

"Arghhhhhhhhhhhhhhhhhh!" Abdul yelled releasing massive amounts of the needle like missiles, each swirled away from his body before forming into an agile beeline toward the island. They continued to slam hard into the force field. Konstanze watched as the other guides only stood and watched the man get closer. Abdul stopped, finally realizing that his attacks were blocked. The man looked to the left, catching movement out of the corner of his eye, and Konstanze looked in the same direction. Aishwarya was there fanatically paddling her small canoe towards them, she was still at least one hundred meters away.

"Death to all that oppose the will of Allah! And to those that rigged my speech to the devils

269

tongue" Abdul shouted releasing a torrent of the jade spirit missiles at Aishwarya.

"Help her!" Konstanze cried out to the guides, who turned to face her after witnessing the attack Abdul conducted on the helpless woman. None of them budged.

Konstanze felt her SES take over and was on top of the spirit beast, her newfound powers almost overwhelmed her as she witnessed she may be too late. As the beams of energy were about to slam into Aishwarya's canoe, she knew she wouldn't make it out to her in time.

"No!" Konstanze could hear Aishwarya scream as she saw the incoming salvo coming from that barbaric Abdul. That's when Max, the American appeared at Aishwarya's side.

"Let's go" Max told the skinny Indian woman, Konstanze watched in disbelief as Max grabbed the woman's hand and they both

disappeared away from the incoming explosion.

"You too" Max appeared at Konstanze's side with

Aishwarya thrown over his shoulder, and hooked

Konstanze off her spiritual mount with his arm.

Konstanze felt as though for only a millisecond, she

was moving through time, as everything got blurry

and slowed down around her. They reappeared back

on the beach next to the other humans; Konstanze

tucked firmly under Max's arm. The Myx Lake

exploded where Aishwarya had just been, causing a

massive purple wave that launched into the sky.

Konstanze wiggled herself free of Max's grip

landing on the ground and stood up rigidly.

Aishwarya beat on the Americans back with her

fists until he plopped her down, butt first on the

ground.

271

"Where is Lazzea?" Serta asked the other guides as Abdul refocused his attention to the island. Like a bull staring at his matador, Abdul stared at everyone on the beach out of his eyes that foamed the green energy.

"Hey Serta, I'm about to take action if you don't" Max said pounding his hand into his fist.

"This guy is out of control," Tesfa commented stepping up besides the American.

"Let's take him out" Bai agreed, also stepping forward. Together all three of the men's SES reacted to their emotions and covered their bodies in energy. Max's was a royal blue while Tesfa's was a Golden yellow, Bai's looked primarily orange but red and yellow were mixed in as well. "Yeah, I'm ready for a little fun" Bai yipped, animated by the idea of the others taking on the fight without him.

272

"None of you will interfere; it is Lazzea's responsibility to detain Abdul at this point" Serta joined the conversation walking over to the human group. All of the humans looked at Serta now who seemed to put himself between them and Abdul.

"What is that?" Aishwarya interrupted. The entire group looked at the Indian woman who was still lying on the ground. Konstanze and the others followed her pointed finger into the sky above Abdul and the lake. An alien flew through the air stalking Abdul, flying stealthily behind the enraged berserker. It had a burnt pink scaly elongated neck that ran out to a black head that had two circular perched eyes on both sides, much like a Chameleon; accompanied by a full mouth of pointed, jagged teeth. It had a muscular body shaped like a praying mantis but with humanoid arms and two leathery pointed wings folded behind its back rapidly keeping it in flight.

"Lazzea is the prime hunter in the Realm" Jazir noted, as the soaring alien darted downward and grasped onto Abdul, plunging the man deep into the lake of Myx, ending the confrontation in a moment.

"Well that settles that for now" Serta brushed his hands together and walked over to the other guides again.

Konstanze looked at the other humans; everyone was on edge about the entire ordeal. Lazzea came bursting out of the lake, his wings flapping in the air and dusting the surface with raindrops of the purple liquid. The large alien smirked, holding the unconscious Abdul in his four fingered hands, Lazzea flew toward the other contestants, finally releasing the Abdul from his grip, and he slammed into the brown beach with an unconscious thud. Lazzea walked to the other guides and once again joined them in conversation.

"Someone should put him in handcuffs," David remarked from behind the group.

"How convenient for you to have an input" Max said smugly to David. Everyone else turned to see the Australian who had vanished the moment Abdul had initially attacked.

"What can I say? I knew what he was capable of." David pointed at Abdul who began to recover on the beach.

"Are you a coward?" Helen piped up, looking back at David as the others anticipated Abdul awakening and attacking. Serta, the smallest of the alien guides walked beside Abdul, observing him. David chose not to respond to Helen. Blowing it off, he walked into the mix, watching Serta and Abdul.

"I'll take him to the hall." Serta said looking at the guides, the small grey alien wearing basic robes saluted the humans, and "I'll see you there shortly." Putting one hand down on Abduls back, Serta and Abdul both disappeared in an instant much like Max had earlier. It almost looked like teleportation.

"So fast," Max laughed to himself as the other guides rallied before the humans.

"We are going to teleport you all at once." Edna said, raising his hands up at them. The other guides moved through the humans and formed a small circle around them. Edna released a zap of energy that flowed in a grey circle around them. Konstanze could feel her body stretched through time and space, pulled to another location. She watched as everyone around her began to twist,

contort and disappearing into thin air, until only her

upper body seemed to remain visible.

Chapter 12: The Hall of Shu

Tesfa landed in the corner of a dining hall that had walls of stone stretching up to a ceiling that wasn't visible. Circular bronze and gold hamlet hung down on silk-like strings giving off a bright enough illumination to reveal Abdul, still unconscious, sitting in one of the eleven chairs at a table made of a hard, wood like substance. Tesfa's eyes began to wander; the other competitors had made it as well. Konstanze, the German, looked like a government worker but carried herself as someone with class would. She stood with her arms crossed staring across at Abdul. Bai, and Max stared each other down; they both seemed petty and prideful. It would be their downfall if Tesfa had to fight them. Catalina, Lucya, Helen, David, and Aishwarya all vomited. They hunched over separately, attempting

279

not to splash the Myx, forcefully ejecting from their bodies, onto their feet; Tesfa looked away. A mixed distortion of colors and body parts began to form and swirl in front of the champions. The guides twisted into reality, teleporting into the room like the humans had just done.

"Are you okay?" Helen asked Aishwarya, trying to comfort the only one that still leaned over, Helen tried to put her hand on Aishwarya's back.

"I am fine!" Aishwarya snapped back, pushing Helens hand away and concealing her mouth with her arm. Helen gave her a disgruntled glare before turning toward the guides.

"Welcome to the Hall of Shu." Serta announced, stepping around the table as he walked up to the other guides. The small grey alien continued, "The Champions of Earth get to feast tonight -- Your host will be Shu himself!" Serta attempted his best to put on a display of show as he spun pointing underhand toward the table. The small alien turned and gave the floor to Edna then proceeded to the other side of the room.

"You have made it thus far, humans; now it's time for your training to begin. You must remember to keep your faith!" Edna smugly clapped his hands together near his head. Stepping forward he continued, "Others before you have come and did not survive the process that is required for your SES to bond with your bodies." The naked yellow alien and Tesfa locked eyes briefly before Edna spun around and followed Serta toward the end of the table.

"The youngest guide among us is three hundred years old; we have seen many tournaments and watched simple beings test themselves throughout this process." Lazzea, the flying lizard

281

grumbled. Tesfa assumed he was the oldest among the aliens. "You must be prepared to test yourselves, humans." Lazzea finished and followed Edna; his wings twitching slightly as he walked.

"What is this, Broadway?" Max tried to interrupt. Tesfa glanced at the American, but the other contestants paid the man no attention. They were interested in the guides inspiring wisdom. Even Bai seemed fixated as Jazir stepped forward.

"There are some of you that have fought and others of you that have never had to throw a punch." The feline humanoid purred, examining each participant. Tesfa noticed she passed over him at the end of the group. As she continued, she seemed to press her piercing cat like eyes into Helen and Aishwarya. "You will now all have to fight. You will all have to kill."

Pike, the last guide stepped forward growling loudly, "We will help guide you and will train you to use your SES. Will you have the courage to defend everything that matters to you? We have seen others make it this far but they shriveled in the arena." He walked to the side and as he did, something else began to take place where he had stood. A large eyeball appeared from nothingness. It blinked at the humans, looking at each of them before spinning. Then a black cloak appeared where the eyeball was.

"What?" Bai managed, putting both of his hands up in a karate stance.

A figure appeared under the cloak that twisted rapidly upward into the room until it stood well over ten feet. A new alien formed but avoided revealing itself; instead, it chose to face away from them as it began a dramatic speech. Its thunderous

283

voice boomed scaring all ten contestants. Tesfa even felt uneasy in the presence of this new individual. "Beings, across the galaxy...the time has come again. I am Shu!" Then the being turned revealing itself.

Bai kept his hands up defensively; Tesfa felt wise doing the same and dropping a leg back in case he head to retreat. The new alien had snow-white skin with light blue veins protruding through a muscular torso that led up to a demonic looking face. Its baldhead had a shape like a hammer, with three softball-sized humanoid eyes that were sky blue. Its eyes glanced over each human moving on their own accord. Shu's mouth opened and closed revealing shark like rows of jagged teeth. "Let the Tournament officially begin with the feast!" Shu gestured toward the table, his muscular white arms motioning for the guests to sit; Tesfa looked over at the table, ahead to Shu.

"This is all really messed up." Max crossed his arms looking at Shu. The others hesitated as well. The alien looked like something from a horror movie. Tesfa decided to lead the way and began to walk to the table; the others followed him timidly. Then two loud vibrating noises, like a drill hitting metal, startled the room. Two large metallic objects unveiled themselves from behind an invisible curtain, right ahead of where the contestants were standing, Tesfa turned as a surprised Bai launched a fiery blast at one of the objects. The motions Bai took were more of a reaction then a full attack. The machine Bai punched went soaring across the room before dully slamming against the wall and landing on the floor. The other machine hovered unthreateningly in place, unaffected by Bai's outburst.

"Bai don't hit the recorders." Shu scolded. Looking at the machine, the alien put his hand up and telepathically lifted the robot with his right hand. With his left hand, Shu spun it through the air directing it at each human. "Now, shall we." Shu looked at the contestants, while the bulky mechanical recorder now floated in midair. The albino alien spun his hand one more time and then pointed at the table. Tesfa felt himself lift up from the ground hovering automatically in air.

"What!" Konstanze yelled, Tesfa looked over and all of the other humans floated in the air magically with him.

"I can't move" David struggled. Tesfa also tried to move but couldn't. All of them now hovered over to the table motionlessly. Tesfa

286

floated right over the table next to seated Abdul.
Each of them hovering lined up with a chair that
they sat in, in unison. Shu himself walked to the end
of the table. His white wrinkled skin on his face
was leathery and they concealed his sunken eyes.

Tesfa sat between Abdul and Aishwarya, the
beautiful young woman from India, who sat on his
right. He could feel Shu relinquished control of his
body and he turned to both sides stretching.

"Who are you?" Lucya didn't hesitate to ask
from the opposite side and end of the table from
Tesfa.

"I am Shu, the first tournament champion
ever and keeper of this realm." Shu pulled out his
large chair and slid himself in comfortably, "The
guides you have met are all past champions that
work for me." Each of the guides stood behind
Shu's chair silently.

"What exactly are we doing here?" Aishwarya asked next and followed up her own question "What if we just want to go home?" The other contestants observed the woman. She was frightened.

"There's no going back Aishwarya." Shu told the woman, "From here on out, you will conform to the tournament rules." At that very moment, Abdul seemed to awaken. Everyone looked at the man as he snorted and opened his eyes. Shu preemptively spun a web around the man.

"Now I think it's time for everyone to introduce themselves." Shu stared intently at Max who sat next to him.

Max looked at the tall white alien who curled his top lip and responded "We already met each other; shouldn't you tell us more about the tournament?"

"There is an order of operations to everything." Shu lectured Max, who looked back at him blankly.

"Well, I think that first and foremost, you should tell us about the tournament." Bai yelled and slammed his fist down on the table; an ash mark where Bai had slammed his fist imprinted itself in the table.

"I will not tolerate insolence or disobedience." Shu stood pushing his chair out and wrapped an imaginary cord around Bai's throat. Bai grabbed at his neck as the other humans watched in fear. Shu went on in a commanding voice "Next time you speak out of line, I will kill you Bai Lo."

Bai clutched at his throat as his face began to turn purple; before losing consciousness, Shu released him from his grasp. Tesfa saw Bai give the alien a defiant cold-hearted stare; he realized Bai

wasn't afraid to fight.

"Don't even think about it." Shu disciplined

Bai once more before the man could rage, "You

have a lot of potential Bai, but if you die here, now,

you forfeit much more than you think." The words

froze the Asian man in his chair.

"I'm Max." Max interrupted as the American

looked around the table, "I'm twenty five years old;

I was born and raised in Detroit, Michigan in the

United States of America." The room's attention

fixated on Max.

"And what is it you do for a living Max?"

Shu asked him curiously.

"I'm a business owner." Max replied

aggressively. Tesfa could tell it was a lie even as

Shu waited for Max to reveal more, but the

American sat there with tight lips looking back at the alien, not giving any further information.

"Okay then, how about you little woman" Shu asked, turning his attention from Max to Helen who sat next to him. Tesfa waited for the English girl to respond. When he had met her, she had been shy and reserved, but she, along with everyone else, seemed very on edge at this table with Shu.

"I'm Helen; I was born in Manchester, England. I'm thirty years old and I'm a Cardiologist at The Guys and St Thomas Hospital." As Helen finished, she looked at Max. Tesfa assumed it probably comforted her somewhat that Max had said he was a business owner.

"I'm happy that you're here Helen." Shu smiled with his rotted green and brown teeth that looked completely inhumane, he went down the line, Bai sat in the middle of the rectangular table.

291

"I'm Bai Lo, I'm thirty three years old and I'm a businessman in Hong Kong, China." Bai finished looking over at Max suspiciously, Tesfa watched as Helen realized that Bai, who was in no way just a businessperson probably, meant that Max wasn't either. The Englishwoman got uncomfortable once more.

"I see; I'm pleased to have you here Bai." Shu bowed his head slightly before motioning for Catalina to speak, who sat next to Max. Tesfa looked across at Catalina. The truth was that every woman here was beautiful but Catalina had a rare beauty. Her dark hair fell down her back and her hazel eyes penetrated the alien before she spoke.

"I'm Catalina, I don't know where or when I was born but I live in Mexico." Catalina casually explained and continued, "I'm a professional thief." The entire table including Tesfa looked at the woman; she looked around at each of them before continuing. "Well I'm not going to lie like those two." Catalina motioned at Bai and Max, "I'm pretty sure they already know who we are, so why be dishonest?" Catalina asked the question to Bai who sat next to her. He didn't respond.

"It is true that we know who each of you are, what you do and have done in your lives, but none of you are on trial here today. Lie or not, the truth will be revealed." Shu spoke up before Max could protest. "How about you?" Shu pointed past Catalina to David.

"I'm David, I'm twenty two years old and I'm an photographer from Gold Coast, Australia." David awkwardly introduced himself in one short sentence; the Australian looked across at Abdul. Tesfa could only imagine having awoken next to the mysterious man forcibly restrained by the guides.

293

The restrained man who tried to attack them began to wiggle and moan with closed lips in his seat. Shu had bound the man's body, limbs and mouth so he had remained relatively silent, but now that David had finished and Shu looked at him, Abdul attempted to cause a ruckus.

"Can you manage to introduce yourself Abdul?" Shu asked the man who only continued in an attempt to wriggle free of his magical restraints. Shu lifted a powder white hand and pinched the air; he peeled back an invisible piece of tape freeing Abduls mouth.

"Death to the infidels who forced me to speak the cursed tongue" Abdul grumbled the words looking at Shu. Shu glanced back at Lazzea.

"You're sure you placed the inhibitor on him?" Shu asked and Lazzea nodded his head in response.

"You cannot stop me; I will destroy all of you in his name." Abdul continued.

"Can you tell us anything about yourself or should I choke you until you turn a different color?" Shu asked without patience.

The room looked at Abdul; he gritted his teeth together looking across at Bai who already experienced being choked.

"My name is Abdul, I was born in Palestine." Abduls words danced on Tesfa's ears as he watched the Middle Eastern man, who could only move his mouth. "I am one of many soldiers in the only true regime in the world, the Islamic Caliphate!" The table all stared silently at Abdul. The Caliphate considered a terrorist organization by many countries worldwide had its soldiers committed genocides in Iraq and Syria; and known to be some of the most ruthless extremists in the world.

Max turned his head and spit on the ground. "Terrorist." Max whispered loud enough for the table to hear. Tesfa felt like saying the exact same thing. Next to him was a radical terrorist; Tesfa had been killing men like him for years.

"What do you know you American dog?" Abdul responded growling the words out, "You live in complete hypocrisy in your forsaken country. You don't even have the fortitude to reveal what you are."

Max stood up prideful taking it as a challenge, "I could have killed you when you attacked us, and I could certainly kill you right now." Tesfa watched as Shu strung Max up with his hand quickly, forcing him to sit back down in the chair. Abdul attempted to spit at Max from in the seat, spraying the table.

Tesfa realized that Shu was now looking at him aiming to switch focuses from the vile Abdul. "I am Tesfa. I'm fifty nine years; I work for the African Union." he said boldly. Looking around the table, he halted at Helen who looked at him horrified in disgust. Tesfa moved on from it and silenced himself as Shu looked at Aishwarya.

"I'm Aishwarya, I'm twenty eight years old and I'm a Professor of Geology and Botany at the University of Delhi." Aishwarya spoke. Tesfa was surprised a teacher was chosen along with him. So far, by what he could tell, no one in the room was as experienced as he was.

"Very nice to meet you, Aishwarya" Shu smiled at the petite woman who returned the grin. Shu looked at Lucya who sat next to Aishwarya,

297

once more, another beautiful woman. She spoke quietly.

"I'm Lucya, I was born in Ukraine but work for the Kremlin in Russia." Lucya chose not to reveal much information about her. That left only Konstanze, the one who rode the fearsome looking spiritual dog.

"I'm Konstanze; I'm a Police Officer; born and raised in Berlin." Konstanze looked around the room, Tesfa noticed the woman never smiled, she had no warmth to her.

"Exquisite! See that wasn't so hard was it." Shu stated looking at everyone; the alien stood up again and clapped his large hands together. "Now let me explain some things you may be wondering." The two large recorders floated through the air on opposite sides of the table until they reached Shu. "Whether you like it or not, you have been chosen to be Earths Champions in the Tournament that will dictate the fate of your world. You may not want to be here, you may not want to train with your SES, and you may not want to have to fight for your life." Shu lectured them, "You were all chosen because of a median of certain attributes our range scanners pick up on: physical strength, speed, stamina, toughness, agility, intellectual aptitude, endurance, flexibility, balance and spirituality. You are the best that your species has to offer, whatever your occupation may be." Shu looked at Max, and then Bai.

"I don't possess any physical strength or speed." Helen held her tiny hands up observing the SES.

"That is why you have one week to train Helen." Shu pointed out, "You will have one week to learn about the strength that you truly possess. That is what the SES will do to you."

"One week isn't enough time to fully train." Konstanze commented.

"One week was all any of us were given, Konstanzc." Pikc remarked from behind Shu.

"Why go through all of this trouble to have a tournament to decide mankind's fate?" Tesfa finally asked. Listening to the others questions or concerns was completely pointless; he felt like the only one that truly understood the gravity of their situation. "Why not just invade and takeover? The Federation has the technology."

"Yes, but unlike humans, The Federation which is a host of many different races, doesn't conquer everything just because it's in our grasp. The galaxy is much larger than you could ever understand." Shu responded, "A species can prove

300

themselves worthy, and continue to evolve much like humans did the last time we visited Earth."

"How many humans survived in the last tournament?" Lucya asked.

"Only two, a great Pharaoh of Egypt and a Greek warrior king; both sat at this very table you sit at now." Shu happily explained. "They were two of the fiercest competitors the tournament had seen in ages. Both put on a great show."

"So just to be clear, this is entertainment for you?" David spoke up from the end of the table, "What are those two things next to you, cameras?"

"Yes, these are called light recorders; they will pick up hundreds of angles all over the room using a projection light technology and have a standard cloaking field built in. They've recorded everything since you've awoken in the Realm today."

301

"Humph" Tesfa snorted, the others seemed to have a similar reaction.

"So you will make us fight for our lives for others amusement?" Helen addressed the alien who looked at her blankly.

"I will personally make you do nothing Helen, but yes, the Federation will force you into the arena if you don't enter at the time willingly. There is much more at stake than your own lives here. You fight for your homes and your planet." Shu answered.

"What is that supposed to mean?" Max asked.

"It means that when a contestant loses they will be destroying parts of Earth, am I correct?" Aishwarya interjected before Shu could continue. The large alien nodded his head in response. "That is evil," she added.

302

Before Shu could go on, Serta interrupted announcing to the room, "Kao Shu, I've just received word from Ra."

Shu grabbed the light recorder to his side; in the lengthy aliens' hands, the device looked miniscule, "You will now see firsthand, the power Platform possesses. The only way to save Earth now is to fight."

Shu spun the recorder and it wandered in full spin to the center of the table before stopping. On both faces of the machine, a projection emerged until each contestant was in a virtual live video feed. Tesfa blinked his eyes rapidly; he was looking down at Earth from space. He must have been viewing this from the recorder in the room. The spinning motion had brought all of them directly into its view port. It was incredibly life like. Tesfa tried to put up a hand to pinch Earth below him, but he had no hand to take action. As Tesfa

looked from right to left without a body, he could

see an expanding tubular structure connected to the

ship, it jutted out from the front and a hot white line

of what looked like Spiritual energy ran through the

middle of it. Tesfa got a chill down his spine, as he

felt something terrible was about to happen.

Chapter 13: James Coventry

Honolulu, Hawaii, United States of America

Tuesday 06/09/15

5:15am

"Alright, are you sure?" Agent pressed the cellular phone against his cheek. The man had been sitting up in his empty bed for two minutes listening to 47 report on how Platform had revealed itself hovering above Tokyo, Japan. He flicked on the television; the gigantic ship was on every channel breaking news. It was dark metallic color, made from an advanced alien species. On the bottom, it took the shape of a decagon, but the aerial view showed a pyramid of glass that stood casting a shadow over the city of Tokyo, Japan. Several massive engines spat a crystal blue flame downward that kept it hovering in place.

305

"Yes, I'm sure. Are you watching it on the television? It's on ever network; people have begun rioting all over Asia" The woman's voice echoed in his ear. Images of the colossal spaceship, rioting in China, Korea, Japan, Taiwan, and Thailand. It made him dizzy pondering the madness this mess would be to clean. "James, are you still there?" 47 asked him.

"Yeah I'm here, just trying to take it all in" he replied lazily. "I have to make some calls," he abruptly finished hanging up the phone. Throughout the later portion of his career, he only allowed a few people to call him James his mate 47, the President of the United States and his mother. James thought about his entire life as he hung up the phone. The invasion of Grenada, The invasion of Panama, The invasions of Iraq, The invasion of Afghanistan, every invasion, every operation, every detail. James remembered everything. His service in the United States Military had begun in 1980 after Vietnam; he joined the Service when everyone else had given up on the ideals of being an American after such a disastrous war. It wasn't until 2009, after James had taken part in every invasion since, that the President had personally visited a then Master Sergeant James Coventry and brought him out to Area 51 in Nevada. It was then that James was promoted, Head of Area 51 Operations, and he learned, no matter how many times the United States invaded, eventually there would be an invasion unlike any humans had experienced for thousands of years. He was fortunate enough to have met 47 while in China investigating something that would change James's life in two ways. The first was 47 became his lover and working partner. The second was the small device they found at a meteorite dig outside Zizang just a couple years ago. He had nicknamed it the

Diplomats Rod after the Koreans had deciphered

the encryption stating it definitely an alien object,

which was given to a human to show they are the

representative of their people. James reached down

under his bed, shuffling around for the foreign

device. He found the tubular object and pulled it up

next to him, it began to glow a violet color, reacting

to his touch.

James put it down next to him on the bed.

With his other hand, he speed dialed one.

"Yes President Henderson, sorry I haven't

returned your call until now. I was on the phone

with my contacts in Asia." James semi lied to Lady

President. He listened to her frantic response; she

needed him there more than ever.

"I'm getting transportation now. I'll be there

shortly." President Henderson responded by

screaming at Agent through the phone something he couldn't make out. Then he saw what the new commotion was on the television. A monumental being at least fifteen feet in height, clad in the same battle armor the other aliens wore, except it had a golden shiny finish, stood on a spaceship deck and talked into the television.

"Earth, I am Ra," the Alien said dreadfully. The camera seemed to zoom in and focus on Ra's armored face. Ra had glowing red eyes and a golden beak attached to his golden robotic armor that extended out like an eagle. Two golden curled horns seemed to protrude out of the top of his head, like the devil himself. "For the first time in 2,000 years, Earth will host the Tournament of the Worlds." Ra continued and Agent watched the television in astonishment.

"Agent! Agent, you need to get me on that spaceship!" President Henderson yelled in frenzied rushed speech, but he could barely hear her. He hung the phone up and focused on the television.

"We look forward to the tournament and at this moment your Champions begin to train with the most advanced weapon technology in the universe, the SES." Ra went on, "At this time we offer you a small preview of those chosen to contend in the games." The camera changed from Ra and an older rock song by the band Kiss began to play.

Agent continued watching the television in disbelief, instantly recognizing the images of each contender as they flashed before him like watching the play by play of a football game. Tesfa Wolde was flying through the air with wings; on the bottom of the screen was a caption of his name and an outline of the Southern half of Africa. Every

310

leader was intensely focused on the worldwide television broadcast.

Russian President Golov sat at his desk watching the apparent introductions of the Champions on the screen. Lucya was on the screen standing on top of a purple river, a pink substance flooded from her mouth and out the sides of her eyes, forming a solid pink elastic shell around her body. A bullet shaped ball shot down a purple river away from the camera, disappearing in an artificial looking jungle. Lucya Konstantinov and a large area encompassing the far Eastern edge of Russia all the way to Istanbul was outlined next to her name.

Chancellor Nimitz rested with one hand on her daughters' shoulder, the other covering her mouth as they watched Konstanze ride atop a brown dog made from the same misty substance Lucya had used to create the ball. The Chancellor read her granddaughters name at the bottom, Konstanze Nimitz and the map next to her highlighted was Europe, from France all the way down to Greece and over to the bottom of Italy.

The usually reserved Australian Prime Minister smiled as David Williams swam like a shark through the purple liquid. Her country was outlined next to it. Proud of her Champion, she picked up the phone to make some phone calls.

Catalina rode on top of a black shadow creature over the lake for President Gomez and his staff's surprise, South America showed up on the television next to her name, Catalina Gonzalez.

President Feng and his staff sat fixated, anxiously staring at the television; Bai Lo appeared to be sprinting upon fire. Bai laughed manically which only added to the suspenseful moment in the room. Next to Bai's name China, South East Asia, China and Mongolia were highlighted.

Prime Minister Landon sat with his legs crossed as he saw Helen drink the purple liquid and the substance come from her eyes and mouth similar to Lucya, the girl from Russia. Helen began to zip down the purple river as if she was rollerblading; Landon shook his head in dismay at the young woman, Helen Hazell, whose caption outlined the United Kingdom and the Scandinavian countries.

The leaders of India, who were on their telephones, watched as Aishwarya floated down the river in her purple canoe. The Indian subcontinent along with Pakistan to Tibet was outlined next to her name: Aishwarya Kapoor.

As Max seemed to teleport distances down the river, President Henderson held her phone

313

against her suit jacket, and watched as the entire North American continent was outlined next to his name: Maximus Smith III.

Abdul Khaleel and an outline of the Middle East, North Africa and Spain launched volleys of unnatural looking green projectiles through the air. The rabid man ran at the other competitors on the screen right before the missiles were about to land devastating them, the screen cut out turning black.

James watched as a black screen with English lettering announced that more would continue shortly from the Tournament of the Worlds. The screen went back to the news showing two news anchors looking shocked, sitting in their chairs talking to each other under their breath, and then immediately broke to commercials. "That could be a predicament," James said to himself as he thought about the last competitor. The phone

314

began to buzz and he looked down to see it was President Henderson again. He answered. "Mam, my apologies" James answered. He listened to the woman go off on the telephone before deciding to hang up again. He quickly browsed through his phone and dialed a number he hadn't dialed in what seemed like ages. "Yes General, yes sir I'm watching now sir, I need emergency transportation to Shanghai, now." James gave the order to the other man on the phone.

Shanghai, China

Tuesday 06/09/15

4:15pm

James Coventry walked into the bottom floor of the Shanghai Tower. 47's real name was Sakura Yumi and she stood at his side. The two

315

held hands momentarily, giving each other a quick look of love before she released his grip to flash her badge to gain secure clearance to a top elevator. As they exited the elevator and entered at the top floor of the massive tower, Agent pulled out his telephone and turned it on for the first time since his flight from Hawaii.

"Are you sure this is what you are going to do, James?" Sakura asked as she walked over to a couch and sat down.

He only nodded to the woman, as he dialed out to the President. "Hello, Lady President." James greeted the woman when she picked up the phone; he decided to put her on speakerphone.

"Where are you Agent?" The President asked at first with concern, and then her professional side kicked in, "I've called you for the last three hours."

316

"President Henderson, if you become the Diplomat to Earth, what does that mean to you?" James asked her directly. A brief pause ensued before the politics of the situation kicked in for the President.

"Our top teams have decided it would be best if I could lead Earth by example and hopefully talk these aliens into sparing the United States of America in exchange for my indefinite service and Earth's infinite gratitude." the President valiantly replied.

Sakura flipped on the television, a recording of Ra's speech and the champion's introduction played on repeat on Chinas leading news channel. "Gratitude isn't going to stop any of this and I don't think it's going to stop this Ra from doing what he came here to do." James replied to the President.

317

"James where are you right now?" President Henderson asked now even further concerned by his disobedient tone.

"That's no longer important madam President you're going to have to put some trust in me..." James began.

"Of course it is, James. You are going to take the position yourself, aren't you? I should have known from the start, you ambitious jarhead. I would have replaced you from the moment I met you if you hadn't had solid footing with the former President...." President Henderson spat at him. James looked over at Sakura, who returned his understanding expression.

"President Henderson, if I were you, I would get on the phone with Beijing and tell them to prepare for the worst possible scenario. Most likely mass starvations or executions. Whatever they do,

318

they must not attack that spaceship; do you understand me? Use whatever leverage you have."

"James, look at this. Something is happening in Beijing." Sakura pointed at the television. James hung the phone up and walked over to where she sat.

"What the hell?" James asked. On the screen, live footage showed a solid white light that shot down from the sky, pulsating as it skimmed over the streets of Tokyo.

"We don't exactly know what is happening, but you are watching live with Tokyo one action news!" The television spoke to him. The camera temporarily looked up into the sky; the light was defiantly coming from the ship.

"They're going to destroy it." James informed Sakura looking down at her.

"Why?" She asked him. The white light began to move slowly from the shoreline, it hit the city and began to comb its way up to the roads and structures.

"A show of strength. They must have done it the first time they came here as well, possibly to an entire tribe of people. Destroy the largest city in the most populated area in the world and you enforce that you want to play fair but if we don't play or play by the rules, this is what will happen."

Sakura looked up at him, "You didn't sound like yourself just now, James." James nodded toward the screen, directing her attention to the live footage. As the light crept into the city, it left nothing behind. Everything that the light touched vanished, no trace of humans, buildings, cars, not even grass rested on a brown dirt blank canvas. The pavement itself had been torn from the earth but it looked as though it had never been there. Sakura put her hand to her mouth in shock, "You have to get up there," she told him.

"I'm about to. Whatever happens from here on out, do everything you can to ensure they don't attack Platform. I'm afraid the Chinese will have no choice. I fear what else is in store for them." James explained to her as he reached in his pocket and pulled out the red disc.

"Are you sure this is going to work?" Sakura asked him, afraid of what he was about to do.

"I've listened to the message a thousand times. I'll be okay Sakura I have a plan. You just make sure you do everything you need to do." James looked at her as he began to walk over to a window on the side of the building; he pulled out a silenced pistol and shot the glass three times shattering it. From the side of this building it would

321

be easy enough for transportation to arrive. He held

out the red disc, and said the words "Yotuka

Barnina Yal Al Salo Ti Shy." Chanting, the disc

vibrated in his hand and seemed to activate. Out the

window from the discs center shot a holographic

image of Ra's head, so real that it looked ghost like.

"This is Ra?" Ra asked looking into the

window, peering from James to Sakura.

"I'm James Coventry of Earth. I am Earths

diplomat and lead ambassador. I humbly wish to

garnish transportation to Platform so I can be of

primary assistance to any and all of the Federations

needs during this great tournament." James

communicated confidently with the holographic

head. Ra seemed to think about the human

presenting himself as Earths Ambassador.

"Very well, James Coventry. Transportation

has arrived at your location; we look forward to

322

meeting you soon." The face of Ra shattered as a black ball fell from the sky propelling itself in the air whistling. A latch shot open on the front and inside the egg like craft, a seat revealed itself. James looked back to Sakura who stood behind him.

"Be vigilant; return to me unharmed. Here is your bag, it has everything you need." Sakura offered him his brown backpack; he took it and without a word jumped from the window to the pod. He spun around to look at her, which he thought could be the last time he would ever see her.

"I love you." She said to him as the door shut.

"Yeah." were his last words. She couldn't hear him say anything, but felt like she knew how he felt. The pod was primarily hollow and dark except for an automatic belt system strapping him in

323

firmly as soon as he sat in the stool-like metallic chair. He could feel the craft move at a bursting speed as it shot up into the air. His backpack, unrestrained, launched up with it hitting him in the face.

The small pod moved incredibly fast and it vibrated James's entire body so much, he could not help but vomit. The sheer force, speed, and momentum made him feel as if his insides were on the brink of rupturing. The pod stopped abruptly, but unfortunately, the vomit fell onto his pants, James looked down dizzy. It was not going to be the greatest look for the Ambassador of Earth, but he didn't have much time to think about it as the pod door unlatched itself. Hosts of aliens were outside ready to greet him; two lines of the aliens varying in size and shape, all clad in the battle armor, formed two rows and two very different figures lurked outside the pods hatch.

"Welcome to Platform I'm Yimb and this is Roewle. Oh my, I knew he would get sick. The last Ambassador from this planet got sick as well." A tall skinny alien with lavender patterned skin and straight black hair that fell down an elongated neck spoke loudly in a female voice. She was wearing fine garments made from a silky material that covered her feminine parts, and an excessive amount of jewelry on her neck, head, and three fingers. The smaller alien, Roewle was pudgy and only stood three feet tall. He had nude colored skin and wore the same silk material clothing as the other. Roewle blinked with its giant round green eyes and looked from James to the taller alien confused. Unlike any of the aliens he had seen so far, Roewle seemed incredibly dull witted and

325

humorous. "Fetch the outfit and some Goiz for our guest!" Yimb announced dramatically, looking at no one in particular behind her. "Come out" Yimb motioned very animated for James to step out of the pod with her jeweled middle finger; he would have already but the straps had yet undone themselves and he had no idea how to get free. One of the battle-clad aliens split the formation behind the duo and jogged up to Yimbs side, the robotic like being held flimsy silk garments in one hand and a clear pail filled with the liquid Goiz in the other.

"Oh! The harness!" The alien exclaimed, clapping her hands together twice. The seat belts unfastened their grip and released James, who fell forward onto the pod floor, only worsening his clothing. James stood up to the best of his ability, walking out of the pod. Yimb held the clothing and a small bucket of liquid out to him, perhaps as a kind gesture.

"Thank you." He took the bucket first setting it down by his side, "Is it safe for me?" James felt stupid after asking such a question; they've already studied humans and he was certain they would not give him something that could cause harm so quickly being he were to represent human kind.

Yimb only nodded her head, and the alien guard that brought the items jogged back to his position in line. "So, do you want me to change here?" James felt Yimb and Roewle both watching him curiously.

"Yes." Roewle nodded his small head and blinked his big eyes, watching James intently; it was nerve wracking having the disgusting little creature watch so closely.

"Well okay." James unbuttoned his first shirt then as he lifted the second above his head, he saw how Yimb and Roewle both examined his every move carefully. Roewle wore a smile on his face that was amusing but at the same time horrifying, James got the inclination the small creature was quiet turned on. He let out a cough while releasing his belt, half expecting them to turn around; neither of them did. It was odd enough having to change on the spot but he would have to wash himself as well. "Are you going to watch me the entire time?" James asked bluntly.

"Oh yessss" Roewle gave the emphasized response nodding his head up and down at a speed that made James feel even more uncomfortable. James looked from Roewles bulged eyes to the elegant Yimb who nodded her head at a slower frequency but stared just as brutishly as Roewle.

328

The man known as Agent, James Coventry slid down his boxers with his pants, there were no further needs for subtleties; sliding out of both shoes, he turned to the tiny puddle of liquid in the container. Dipping both easily into the watery substance, he washed himself as quickly as he could. Putting on the clothing given to him was quite a different situation; as soon as he felt the lime green shirt and white pants with his hands, a strange sensation took over his fingertips. The clothing fit much like sweatpants and a cotton tee shirt, but the sensation that it gave felt like tiny drops of warmth crawling slowly over James's entire body. It was the finest material he felt in his entire life. James looked over at Roewle and Yimb who watched the entire process with joyful smiles.

"Do you feel better?" Yimb asked.

"I do, thank you. What is this material?" James asked plucking one of the sleeves of the shirt and watching it fall down slowly wrapping around his skin.

"It's called Shisoul; each piece of the clothing is drenched in the blood of a child Marshi from the planet Wex," Yimb explained the horrifying twist. James went from examining the pants to looking back at Yimb in dismay. Roewle began bouncing forward in an unthreatening manner, without saying a word and grabbed James' leg in a hug causing James to tense up unsure of what to do.

"Welcome to Platform, Ambassador Coventry." Roewle greeted James in a high-pitched cute voice, changing the subject. Looking up at James, Roewle smiled a frightening smile; the oversized dull buckteeth on the creature were truly scary.

"Alright we should get going so we can start the meeting. Ra and the others are in the Primary Bay, which isn't a very great distanced from here." Yimb held out her ridiculously skinny arm and turned around, beginning to walk down the line. Roewle released James's leg and bounced behind him, plucking his backpack up from the pods floor. James watched as the alien taste tested his previous lunch, before following in Yimb's footsteps. James had no other choice; he cautiously followed his two hosts. James continued following silently behind Yimb and Roewle as they led him through the rows of armed soldiers until it finally ended and they approached a solid platinum squared metallic structure. On the wall was a square fenced in device that resembled a super computer; it stood solo in the

331

middle of the square. Yimb and Roewle both walked through a gate that Yimb unlatched and waited as James joined them where they stood.

"Primary Bay One" Yimb leaned down and placed her hand on a ball like pad, activating the transportation system.

"Primary Access granted Titan Yimb Dullah." The computer lit up with lights and gauges; underneath the pad, a smoke material leaked out from both sides. Before James could sturdy himself, the pad displaced all three of them. He could feel his body being sucked through space and he closed his eyes as he twisted into a new location. He fell to the new pads floor onto both knees; looking down at the metallic surface underneath he paused to catch his breath.

"Are you okay Ambassador?" Yimb asked James, who managed to look up. The site before him was remarkable. Several beings sat around a circular smooth table with different sized seats. On the table was a smooth oddly shaped projector system that ran a live feed of specific events. He concluded they were definitely somewhere near the edge and top of the craft. As he looked to the left, away from the table, he could see massive lightly tinted windows, which revealed a spectacular lighted oddity outside of the ship, to the likes James had never seen.

James diverted his attention from outside when he heard his name being called by none other than Ra, the massive being he saw and heard on the transmission earlier today. "James Coventry, the Ambassador." Ra stood up from the biggest seat at the table. He was every bit as terrifying as James imagined him to be from what he had seen on television. Ra was at least fifteen feet in height and clad in his golden battle armor that shined brighter on one side from the light just outside of the ship. "Welcome to Platform." Ra welcomed him in a deep voice. The beak of the armor opened like a mandible revealing the helmet that Ra wore was unlike what the aliens who had captured the Champions were wearing; Ra's was built directly onto his face.

"Come, join us." Ra extended his hand offering James an empty seat at the table before sitting back down at the head of the table in a massive chair made only for a colossal humanoid. James walked over, Yamib and Roewle on each side of him. As he got closer to the table, he could see more clearly through the rectangular windows what was happening outside. He stopped in his tracks and opened his mouth in fright at the atrocity. A clear tubular structure beaming a fluorescent white light ran parallel with the direction James faced as he wandered aimlessly toward the window. Staring in disbelief as a child would at an ice cream truck passing them by on a hot summer's day; James wandered closer to the light. It became startlingly more surreal when he finally reached the window; he could hear Yimb, Roewle, and Ra walk up casually behind him, and saw their reflections as they all looked outside. It wasn't a tube at all, as the object appeared to be on his television instead it was a perfectly smooth massive opaque colored crystal shooting down a white beam onto the planet below.

"What do you think, Ambassador?" Ra questioned James as he approached, "It's one of Platforms mightiest weapons, The Lark. I control it directly with my energy."

"It's incredible," James replied in fear, as his heart seemed to sink into his stomach. Yimb and Roelwe smiled and watched the weapon carve like a knife into the planet below. "What exactly is it doing?" James asked.

"Here take a closer look." Ra handed him a cylindrical telescopic device and James readily pressed it tightly to his eye. It was, as he had feared; he saw thousands of Chinese bodies floating through various amounts of debris, lifelessly without oxygen twirling through space, sucked into the light like a vacuum.

Chapter 14: Pairing Up

"What the hell is going on?" Abdul kept
saying but he couldn't tell if his words were coming
out. He was no longer in his body; instead, he was
watching a massive white light sucking thousands
of corpses, building debris, and cars through space.
He floated there without body. "What the hell is
going on?" Abdul repeated, seeing the dead brought
up flashbacks of the war in Syria. Abduls mind
raced but he couldn't tell if this was all in his head
or if he was really experiencing this nightmare.

"Get me out of here!" Abdul heard one of
the women cry again. Apparently they could speak.

"Get me out of here!" Another woman
shouted desperately, the Indian girl.

"Please, Allah! Get me out of here!" Abdul
cried as he watched an infant fly close to his face,

he tried to reach out to push the child away but discovered he had no hand to push with. Suddenly, Abdul snapped back into his body when he heard a loud clicking noise. He immediately looked around the room, two of the other women, Helen and Aishwarya were recovering but everyone else's eyes had gone white. The white alien known as Shu stood at the end of the table observing a tiny portable electronic device. His bindings still invisibly grasped onto Abduls hands waist and legs rendering movement useless.

"Get me out." David, the Australian man cried out across from him. Abdul looked at him in fear. The machine floating in the middle of the table popped, and Abdul watched as David hunched over in his seat gasping for air. Five minutes later, everyone had recovered from the devilish machines teleportation technique. Some of the women and men cried. Abdul watched as even the tough looking Asian man shed tears over the dead. Abdul felt no such remorse.

"What did you think?" Shu broke the silence in the room, as he looked to each human.

"What was happening out there?" Max asked looking at Shu sternly.

"The same thing that will happen to each of your homes if you're not successful in this tournament" Serta answered the question from behind Shu's chair.

"So many deaths" Bai cried, a tear rolling down his face silently. Aishwarya sat in her chair with both hands on her face sobbing.

"I don't want to do this, I never asked for this," Helen anxiously spoke out also in a nerve-wrecked state.

"You must stand strong Helen; there will be no room for weakness here," Tesfa tried reassuring the English woman.

"It may be easy for you. You're a murderer, I've never killed anyone." Helen snapped at the man. Tesfa was taken aback by her words. She hadn't been spiteful towards him until now.

"This is extinction were talking about," David remarked wiping away the last of the wetness on his face.

"Exactly" Shu replied, everyone looked at him now, "That is exactly what it will be if you don't fight for your planet."

"You are a monster," Aishwarya screamed at him, "Monster!"

"No. I was once in your very shoes," Shu began, "I have seen worlds come and go girl. Let me tell you, if this is your constant attitude, you will not survive and neither will anything you have ever loved."

"We are not just some god damn entertainment to be played with in a game," Bai barked.

"But you are. This is the Tournament, the biggest game of all," Jazir now commented stepping forward, "The best thing about games though Bai, and you know better than most is, you can win."

"Why though? Why did you have to kill so many people?" Lucya asked; she seemed rather unconcerned with the deaths. She and Konstanze remained the composed women at the table while Helen, Catalina, and Aishwarya made soft depressive sounds.

"Believe it or not, the last time we were here on Earth, we destroyed that exact same city," Shu mumbled an unsatisfactory answer.

341

"So you destroyed it again?" Max asked smugly, "None of this makes sense."

"It became a tradition. Ra makes the decisions, and I ensure the contestants get trained" Shu said with finality, putting a stamp on the subject.

"I would love to meet this Ra," Bai managing his emotion commented, pressing his hand hard against the table.

"What you all really need to do is ask yourselves right here and now if you can do this. It won't get any easier from here on out" Pike said, joining the conversation and stepping forward with the rest of the guides.

Abdul had remained silent throughout the complaints and tears; he had no love for any of these other people as he watched the Indian woman cry. He may have to calm down for now if he wants to survive this entire bout. That would mean that he would have to remain sharp and work his way in with these people for now. Sooner than later he would get the opportunity to strike on any non-believers and with his new powers, he would be assured access into Heaven when he disposed of their bodies like the ones he had seen in space. Aishwarya stopped crying and everyone looked at Shu again. Abdul shifted his attention as well.

"Shu." Abdul addressed the abdominal creature gaining its attention before it spoke again, "I realize the error in my ways. Attacking these people wasn't right for me to do. Can I please get unbound at this point?"

"Well, that was sudden. What's with the change of heart, slick?" Max asked from the other end of the table. The others didn't understand the rude and arrogant remark. Abdul chose to ignore the rudeness.

"After seeing the many dead children, I realize I would never want that to happen to my loved ones or any of your loved ones. I think we all need to work together to make sure it doesn't happen," Abdul said cheekily. The others looked at him before David chose to make a cut into his dramatic faked mood change.

"Liar! You're a liar and I don't feel comfortable with you moving on your own." David leaned onto the table looking across at Abdul in the eyes as he gritted his teeth together. The Australian man was very sharp, picking up so quickly on Abdul's act.

"Give the man a break, he made a mistake," Tesfa spoke up for Abdul. Abdul turned his head as much as he could to look at the black man, like everyone else instantly had.

"You have got to be kidding me," Konstanze sarcastically said to Tesfa.

"I agree. It is time for Abdul to adjust himself to being a champion of Earth," Shu remarked and as he swirled his hand around in a small circle Abdul felt the magical binding's release. He looked around the room thinking that at this moment if he put everything he had into it, if he focused all of his spiritual powers onto the detonation and strictly became the explosive, he may be able to take all of them with him. Abdul locked eyes with Shu who stared at him.

"First, you will all eat. You must be famished," the tall alien arose in his seat and clapped three times. The sounds were thunderous booms instead of normal claps. After Shu clapped

345

food, plates, glasses, beverage containers and silverware appeared. "Eat, then you will pair off and travel to the five training fields in Rol with a guide." Abdul could feel his stomach turn over; he was hungry indeed. Anticipating an alien delicacy, Abdul was relieved to see large portions of human food, though exotic to his eyes. "This will be your last human meal. The remainder of your time here you will learn how to forage and hunt down your own food at the training grounds," Shu announced. Every contestants looked at the food hungrily.

"Is that mashed potatoes?" Max asked grabbing the first bowl and starting a feeding frenzy. Each person received potatoes, steak, green beans, peas, salad, fruits, cheeses and desert until their bellies were full, and Abdul ate until he was filled to the brim.

Shu sipped on a mug filled with a strange grassy tasting liquid they all had been drinking. "Now, let's talk about the pairings. You must decide on your own and I will assign a guide best suited for each pair," Shu interrupted the last of their meals.

"Oh, Lucya!" Max suggested looking at the woman across from the table.

"Oh, sorry Max. I think I'm going to pair with Konstanze." Lucya nodded her head at the German woman who gave her an accepting expression back.

"When did you decide that?" Max argued, but Catalina interrupted him.

"Max, I'll partner with you." Catalina said, admiring the man, she seductively put emphasis on her words to persuade the man.

"Okay." Max replied bluntly, checking her out. Abdul could tell the American was a standard dog, but he couldn't help but feel envious. None of these people would want to pair with him after he tried to kill them so suddenly.

"We should probably pair together." Aishwarya informed Helen quickly, as each pair formed.

"Actually I don't think that's the most splendid of ideas." Helen quietly replied to Aishwarya, who looked devastated by the rejection, "David, will you be my partner?" Helen asked the Australian. There went Abduls only shot at a stable partner as David nodded, accepting Helen. Aishwarya seemed infuriated by Helens decision but held her tongue.

Bai, the Asian man, chose her boldly over Tesfa or Abdul. "Aishwarya, you will come with me." Bai looked sternly at the woman. Afraid of being disobedient or having to accept Abdul himself as a partner, Aishwarya agreed, nodding her head.

"Well that leaves you and me, Abdul." Tesfa looked over to him with a calm look, too calm for Abdul's tastes.

"Yes, I guess it does." Abdul responded, Tesfa was the eldest in the room, Abdul could tell. It would be hard to pull the wool over his eyes.

"Are you okay with that Tesfa? I'll go with him if you want." Max questioned Tesfa. Abdul growled at the notion and was about to say something but Tesfa spoke again with speed.

"It will be okay. He has repented for his earlier actions. I'm confident that we will be the best training partner at this table." Tesfa encouraged Max and the others then gave Abdul a devious nod.

"Yes, it will be a death match, you and your God will burn on the mantle of Allah," Abdul agreed mumbling the last bit under his breath before putting his hand to his mouth in surprise. Shu seemed pleasantly surprised at the fact that the humans all agreed.

"Wonderful!" Serta clapped his hands together, very humanoid like.

"Nothing like Guangwu or Octavius" Shu praised as well, "Serta you will go with Tesfa and Abdul." Before Abdul could blink, Serta stood behind them and put his hands on each of their shoulders.

"Shall we, humans?" Serta asked. The little grey demon terrified Abdul for the most part, but for now, he would accept his fate. It all happened suddenly. Abdul felt his body twist into the nether once more as Serta pulled them through time and space. He became nothingness and his body became empty of everything. "Welcome to the Crat." Serta mused as they reappeared in a different location, sitting on the ground. Abdul opened his eyes carefully and looked around; nothing of this place would be spared once he could fully harness the weapon Allah had bestowed upon him. The black short grass they sat on was an abomination, the orange sky wasn't one of his creations, and the giant multicolored trees shaded yellow and brown that surrounded them were not from his kingdom. Serta was a demon, Tesfa was a lost soul, they would not be spared Abduls wrath.

"We begin training with your SES starting now; I hope you both are prepared." Serta said methodically, "But first I need to explain a little more about the transformations that you will go through."

351

"Transformations?" Abdul asked aloud, looking at Serta questioningly.

"Yes, your body will no longer require sleep while in this Realm." Serta explained and went on, "So, for the next two days, we will practice basic sparring sessions with each other."

"Wonderful, absolutely spectacular" Tesfa replied. Abdul could feel the other man's eyes on him.

"Now, if you could both stand still while I..." Serta began, and then disappeared from Abduls eyesight. Abdul tried to bounce back and react as he realized the alien was behind him but there was no time. Serta stabbed another device into the center of Abduls back and disappeared again, doing the same to Tesfa. Suddenly the grey alien stood again in front of them. It all happened in mere seconds.

"What was that?" Tesfa roared, reaching with his hands to his back, trying to snag the device with his fingers; Abdul mimicked him attempting to touch whatever it was. There wasn't any pain as the device sunk deeper into his ski. It gave him a light tingling, burning sensation.

"It's a Birk modular attachment constructed on the Titan moon and distributed only to competitors in the tournament." Serta informed them. They both looked dully back at him, and he knew they didn't understand. "It's a device that will allow you to train to the fullest of your potential."

"Like the purple stuff?" Abdul asked, wondering about the strange liquid. When Abdul had consumed it, he had felt invincible, as if he could destroy anything. Although he had been naive at that time, he would capitalize on anything that would give him an advantage.

353

"No. This is unlike Myx; you won't be sparring under the influence of any type of spiritual enhancer." Serta mumbled, "Everything will be clear soon enough. For now take what defensive positions you will to duel each other." Serta walked in between them and motioned with his hands for them to separate. Tesfa turned and walked about twenty feet away from them.

"Is this a proper distance?" Tesfa asked Serta. It wouldn't matter the distance. If Abdul were asked to fight this man, he would kill him here and now.

"I leave it up to both of you. The field that we're in is the exact same size of the arena. In human measurement, it's about equivalent to a football field," Serta yelled across the grass to Tesfa, who backed up a couple more steps. "Use the trees that surround us as your walls. Use this

354

field as your battleground. During this first fight, I'll judge both of your abilities and we will work from there."

Abduls blood began to boil as he looked across at Tesfa. The darker man stared right back at him in a showdown of eyes. "And begin!" Serta announced and hopped out of sight. The words panicked Abdul, who looked intensely at Tesfa who kept taking more steps back. Did the man not intend to fight him? It seemed like he was going to run away. Maybe he was scared having seen Abdul's capability.

"I will show you no mercy," Abdul said the words under his breath, smirking. Abdul could feel the spiritual power pour out from his fingertips and the sides of his eyes; the green color of the chosen flag of Islam was no surprise at all to Abdul. It would be the last color the man across from him would see before his death. A tube of the green spiritual mist formed solid on Abduls shoulder. He grabbed the middle of it and with an extreme hatred and aggression; he began building up the power he would release. The grass around him swayed as his power took form. Tesfa continued backing up. He must see what is coming but he wouldn't be able to stop him in time. Abdul fired the first shot. It propelled out of the tube, just as he had anticipated. A swarm of forest green spiritual blades sliced through the air at Tesfa from his head to his feet. Abdul watched his perfect creation fly at its target and miss as Tesfa sprouted the golden mythical spiritual wings and dodged at the last second. Abduls projectile had missed. He fired three more simultaneously, his body bucked back with each shot. It was amazing to watch the man dodge all three shots from his canon. At first, Tesfa shot up

356

and around, then to the other side, doing a barrel roll in the air.

"Are you just going to dodge me?" Abdul roared out, though the green moisture permeated uncontrollably out of his eyes, as he looked across at the silent Tesfa, who stood there with his wings flapping slowly. He seemed to be entirely at ease.

"I don't need to dodge you to beat you." Tesfa replied arrogantly. It infuriated Abdul to watch the man stand there so smug. He had backed himself to the edge of the bowl that the trees created. This next barrage he wouldn't be able to dodge. He would launch the seeking missiles and nothing would be able to shield the man.

"Do you know why?" Tesfa continued antagonizing. It only made Abdul angrier. "Because you are the son of the devil, and I've seen what you can do. I'm your partner so I can destroy you, Lucifer."

Abdul put his hand on the dark ground in a rage, and watched as his power amplified and began to build behind him in a cloudy haze. The pin like spiritual bullets began forming at three feet around him and began to spread out behind. "Arghhhhhh!" Abdul screamed viscously as the SES caused the green power to ooze from his mouth. He moved forward, walking at a steady pace in Tesfa's direction. The green projectiles he conjured multiplied repeatedly and spun in place midair. Abdul took a step forward, each of the green rods move with him. Tesfa remained in place. One hand glowed golden ahead and one hid behind in a sideways stance. Abdul would cover the entire tree line with these blasts. There wasn't anywhere for the man to run. Abdul lunged forward with a big leap, making it an entire quarter of the way to Tesfa. The pins of energy behind him launched themselves at Tesfa, following Abdul's lead. They shot ahead bursting through the air and Abdul could see through the chaos, Tesfa reveal his other hand. He was holding a golden book.

"Genesis Chapters six through nine." Abdul heard Tesfa preach the biblical words, and as he did from behind the African, coming through the tree, Abdul saw something horrifying. It phased through Tesfa's body as if he were a ghost, but it was as solid and real as anything Abdul had ever seen, "The Ark!" Tesfa yelled out. It encompassed his entire view, and dwarfed his weapon barrage he had launched at Tesfa. Abdul watched in dismay as his green pins hammered into the bow of the giant golden boat that stammered forward through the air unaffected by the blasts.

Now Abdul had to run but his body felt drained. He couldn't move his feet. He fell sideways onto the grass and turned around to see the massive ship strewn from Tesfa's spiritual energy, gliding closer to him. Abdul began crawling; he would never make it away from an attack that massive in size. The ship seemed to lock onto Abdul as he tried to scuttle away, and he felt as the edge crashed into his back. The spiritual power burst all around him as the ship continued to pound into his back. Trapped under the immense force he could feel his spinal cord snap under the weight, he didn't even have time to get last words out, only a muted scream. He continued to yell in pure agony. Abdul screamed at the top of his lungs as he felt the behemoth weight of the spiritual density. It crashed into him and only continued to flood into his body and the ground as it exploded. Abdul lost

360

consciousness somewhere in the middle of the ship

and as everything seemed to slip away, he could

feel his eyes roll into the back of his head, and knew

he was about to die.

Chapter 15: The Deadly Duels

"Stand up Bai, you okay?" Edna asked, the alien approached him as he lay there looking into the empty orange sky. The last thing he could remember was Aishwarya slicing him with the vines that had come up out of the ground like whips. He could do nothing to stop her at that point it appeared the fight was finished.

"I'm so sorry!" Aishwarya sat on the ground ten yards from him crying anxiously, with her hands on her legs and her head in lap. "I don't know what happened, it all occurred so quickly," she panted the words breathing deep breaths.

"Did I die?" Bai looked up at Edna who had disappeared before his and Aishwarya's duel.

"You did. The Birk Modular connects directly to your SES and is amplified in this

Realm." Edna began to explain the strange contraption he had jammed in each of their backs. Bai reached around again to touch the device but had no such luck, "It will repair any deadly damage taken to your body, no matter how mangled, sliced or even ripped apart your body may be," Edna laughed saying the last part.

"How would that work with a person that's decapitated? You'd have to assume their head and body parts would have to remain attached," Aishwarya asked in amazement.

"You may end up finding out, but first let's talk about what happened with you both in your duel," Edna proposed.

Bai rubbed his face looking over at the shaken Aishwarya. The woman had gone all out in fear of his attacks, when she had said at first that she wouldn't fight. He looked at her sitting across

from him in the clearing. The place that Edna had
called Sunspot was high up on a circular mountain.
He looked behind him, for miles all he could see
was the cream-colored orange sky and the exotic
colored tree line. He would have to be careful not
to push the woman over the edge.

"Listen." Bai yelled across the tanned rocky
desolate surface to the woman, "I don't find any
discomfort in hitting a puppy."

Aishwarya looked wearily down at the
ground. She clearly didn't want to be here, or fight
Bai for that matter. "I never asked to be here. I
have never fought in my life," she called out to him
in resistance.

"But you heard what that yellow bastard
said. We have five minutes to start or he will come
down and punish us both," Bai yelled out.
Aishwarya recoiled in intimidation. It wasn't what

he had meant to do to the woman, but her hesitance was wearing him down.

"If you don't fight me, I will hurt you." Bai tried calmly saying across the mountaintop, "You will need to defend yourself. Here I come." The blazing hot energy, a mixture of yellows, reds, and oranges that ultimately made it look like fire, began to seep from Bai's eyes as he looked across at the woman. He had grown accustomed to the burning feeling, like an ink master's needle to his skin; the spiritually driven power also gave him a thrill of painful satisfaction.

"I don't want to do this!" Aishwarya protested as she observed him. To her, he must look terrifying. He couldn't help but smile.

"Too late, it's time to test these things out." Bai came at her. In his right hand, he could feel his power leak from his fingertips and begin to spin in his palm. He would launch one close to her to let her know he wasn't playing a game with her. The energy in his tingling hand crackled as it formed into a dense swirling fiery mass spanning a few feet in circumference. He threw this one with only fifty percent of his strength. Years of little league baseball playing for Boss Zhang did not pay off, as his aim didn't align. The fireball that crackled and wafted through the air headed straight for the woman frozen like a deer in headlights. "Dodge!" Bai declared loudly. As he watched, the woman had plenty of time but she stared unmoving at his attack until at the very last second before impact, the woman jumped out of the way. Nevertheless, her arm was scorched by the gaseous sphere.

Aishwarya looked petrified at her arm. From her shoulder to her elbow the flesh was burnt. The skin bubbled in certain areas. "You self-serving jerk." Aishwarya screamed in tears at Bai from across the arena shaped dueling grounds. Bai didn't feel any guilt; he wanted to perfect his attacks for the real battles.

"You can't expect me to go easy on you even if you don't want to be here!" Bai rebutted sternly, in both of his hands two more of the fireballs began to form. He felt as though he was allowing her to buy time but he continued, "I never asked to be here either, but now that I am, I'll do everything I can to live." The balls of energy in each of his hands began to burn his palms; he had to release them soon. A line of sweat seemed to melt on Bai's face; the heat his energy permeated was so hot that he didn't understand how his skin hadn't simply disintegrated. "You will have to fight, Aishwarya." Bai growled, launching both of balls of energy from his hands, one after the other by performing straight punches.

The woman hadn't recovered from the burn she had suffered from his previous efforts to get her attention. She looked in horror at the two incoming blasts moving much faster than his last. Then Bai saw her finally react. Her power was unlike his. It didn't flow from her hands or come from her eyes. Instead, it formed wrapping around her feet into a teal solid globe. The Earth shook underneath Bai and he looked again at the woman. The entire ground under her seemed to shift, in between Aishwarya and the fireballs the ground spiked up, forming a tan rocky wall. Both of Bai's blasts burst against the wall that shook, extinguishing themselves. He peered behind the wall at Aishwarya, who seemed to be doing something to her arm. Almost magically, the burn mark vanished, and the woman looked up at Bai with wild eyes.

"Will you kill me Bai?" Aishwarya asked from behind the rock wall.

"If I have to, woman." Bai barked. He was sick of holding back. She must have an affinity with the Earth much as he must with fire. If that was the case, he would have to get close to her or she may block again as she just did.

"I don't want to die." She responded and disappeared from his vision, jogging behind the wall of rock.

He would no longer allow her to delay. He built the energy in his feet and launched himself into the air and like a wingless bird; he flew above the barrier, and landed gracefully in her previous location. "If you don't want to die you will have to fight me." Bai proclaimed, recovering from his landing and looking at the woman. The energy in the corner of his eyes came to life as he began to build up another attack.

"I'm so sorry," Aishwarya apologized looking down at the ground below Bai, "I don't know what's about to happen but I don't want to die."

Bai hadn't realized he had walked right into a trap until he looked down at the ground to see the rocks were covered with small teal beads. Then solid teal vines burst out of the ground rhythmically shooting themselves into the air and through his body, piercing right through his calf, his abdomen and his back.

"Screw you!" Bai screamed in agony. He looked at Aishwarya, whose face was covered in small tears. More of the vines kept shooting out from the ground, stabbing through him until he was unable to move.

"I'm so sorry!" Aishwarya squeaked her words were nearly blocked out under his murderous yelps of pain.

Bai's body hung there by the many vines that had torn him to pieces. He looked at Aishwarya one last time, "Damn tyke," he managed to cough out some blood. Seconds later, he lost consciousness.

"Bai Lo, in your first duel you claimed to lack empathy but chose to casually attack your foe with a deep fear that you would harm her." Edna explained standing over him. Bai touched his skin in each of the places the vines had ripped into him. Everything seemed normal as though it had never happened.

"What do you expect? She was feigning distress," Bai responded. The more he thought about the first duel, the angrier he got. At this point, she had seemed to trick him.

"I feigned nothing; I did not want to die." Aishwarya argued, upset at the notion.

"Damn it" Bai shouted at the girl, but Edna began speaking once more before he could scold her.

"Bai, you have a natural instinct about you and an incredibly rare multi colored SES. It gives you the potential to be the strongest fighter in this entire tournament but you must learn to truly harness your strength." Bai looked at Edna. For the first time, he was interested in the multi colored energy only he seemed to possess. It gave him a feeling of uniqueness.

"Aishwarya, in this tournament most of the time you will not have time to devise plans or to prepare for your opponents attacks. Your first fight you showed courage by luring in your opponent and utilizing your knowledge to create a defensive strategy that worked in your favor," Edna praised her, "But you must learn to be vigilant when it comes to pressing the attack. You will not be shown mercy when it comes time for a real battle, I assure you that," Edna finished looking back at Bai.

"I don't want to do this at all! I was fighting to survive," Aishwarya shouted at Edna. The yellow alien's bulbous face turned back to the Indian woman who sat panting on the ground. "Did you see what I did to him?" she asked them both, still in bewilderment about what she had achieved.

The words stung Bai who took them personal, "You won't have to worry. Next time it will be you waking up from the dead," Bai disclosed giving the woman a menacing look.

"I don't want to do this," Aishwarya whimpered again. At this point, Bai ignored the girl's cries. They were nothing more than false melodies he couldn't stand listening.

"Well done, shall we start then Bai?" Edna asked quickly. Bai looked up at Edna from the ground. He hadn't moved since awakening from the traumatic experience.

"We are going to duel again right now?" Bai asked bluntly, attempting to stand. The wounds were still recovering and he heard several of his bones and joints pop together as he rose.

With very little effort, literally moving his hands only a tad, Edna flattened Aishwarya's jutted rock structure. It lay evenly with the ground once more. "Yes right now. For the next two days you

375

will fight, eat, and fight more," Edna confirmed, now looking at Aishwarya who still sat in a submissive state.

"Will we be wearing the Birk Modular during the actual tournament?" the woman asked Edna meekly. Bai could read on her face that killing him had really taken its toll mentally, but he could not show any further weakness.

"Ha, Ha." Edna laughed strangely, "What a silly question."

"I'll take that as a no," Aishwarya said standing up to her feet again; she looked Bai in the eyes now. "You can't go easy on me or I'll beat you every time." Aishwarya challenged him, or at least that's how he interpreted her words.

Bai began a steady jog away from her and Edna, "We will have to see about that. Don't get cocky; you tricked me last time."

376

"Don't call me names you little prick. My name is Aishwarya," she corrected him backing up to the other side of what would become their battleground. At least the woman had found enough nerve to fight him. Bai felt a bit of pride as he jogged further. The distance he had leapt to reach the woman in their fight was much further than any of his leaps when he was hopped up on the purple liquid. His body felt new, as if no harm had come to him at all. He reached the other side before spinning to face his opponent once more.

"Okay" Bai jested, his spirit returned to him as he looked at the woman he was about to kill, "If you beat me one more time, I'll call you by your real name." Bai shouted out to her mockingly, "But until then, you are just another flea bitten wench." Aishwarya gave him a look of contempt from across the way. A gentle breeze blew in from behind Bai,

377

and the spiritual energy began to build around his eyes.

"Begin." Edna yelled before disappearing. This time Bai didn't need any encouragement. He began building up the pressure in both hands and feet, he was going to go at the woman full force.

"Here I come, Aishwarya!" Bai yelled, building up more power. Unlike before, he allowed his temper to flare and the oranges, yellows and reds swirled around his body like fire in a tornado. Aishwarya looked across at him. He knew this time he would be the victor; she wouldn't be able to stop him. Bai let out a hideous war cry lunging forward at the woman. He wouldn't hold back at all this time, she was toast. Instead of hiding or holding back, Bai realized the woman was also making a direct beeline for him from across the battleground; her arms were enshrouded with her teal spiritual

378

energy. It got him even more excited that she was ready to do battle and he moved at an even brisker pace with his head narrowed at his target. Bai pounced forward twenty yards from the woman, he thrashed with a punch wrapped in his fiery spirit, and aimed for Aishwarya's face. The fireball itself seemed to suck all of the spiritual energy around Bai in as it moved at incredible speeds from his enclosed fist. Aishwarya saw the projectile and with both her hands, she pumped sideways, her arms extended out into the solid teal vines that stabbed Bai before. The woman used the momentum to barrel roll sideways through the air and escape Bai's attack. She landed hard on the ground not far from him on her stomach; Bai felt himself hesitate before he snapped out of it. She was taking the time to recover; Bai built the energy up in both of his feet and pounced forward through

379

the air while building up more energy in his right hand.

"Aishwarya!" Bai yelled in the air, half because he wanted to warn her but the other half purely out of killing instinct. His fireball shot straight from his hand as he closed in on her. She looked up in time but didn't recuperate quickly enough.

Chapter 16: Fairoh; The Arena of Arhgripye

Lucya barely dodged Konstanze's brown snarling energy beast she rode a top. Most of their battles consisted of the German chasing the blonde haired Lucya around their dueling grounds and Lucya reacting to the superb offense.

"They're getting much better" James suggested, sitting on an incredibly comfortable piece of blue furniture looking at the enormous rectangular monitor Lucya and Konstanze did battle on. Yimb tinkered with an electronic heating device in her cooking room; they were inside her home in the Metropolis Arhgripye, an apartment complex that shot several hundred stories into the air. James had learned quickly that anyone with the Titan status like Yimb possessed, were treated like

381

royalty. The apartment where James had taken residence with the female alien and her companion Roewle was located so far off the ground it was no longer visible from the open windows that gave a staggering view of the chaotic city. James took a minute to look out the window. Skywalks connected all of the massive buildings. Pods of all different shapes, colors and sizes, much like the one that had picked him up and briskly transported him here, zoomed through the sky providing transportation for the hundreds of different alien species. Only the Titans were permitted to use the teleportation pads, which is how they had avoided another debacle with his stomach.

"Yes, they are Ambassador" Yimb replied sourly. "You've watched them eat, hunt, sleep, and fight for nearly an entire day. How much longer will you babble for?"

"Well, we want to make sure everyone is in top condition for the tournament don't we?" James asked Yimb, manipulating the situation so she couldn't go any further. His alien host had originally seemed to like and care for him, then treated him with traces of hostility since Ra had informed her that he would be staying in her quarters with Roewle.

"Yes, this is true" Yimb stammered over the plate she was holding. Although she may be agitated with James, she had ended up being an incredible host, catering to any of his needs. "So, a day has gone by and you've watched all of them. Who is the best?" she asked handing him the plate. He gladly accepted it and set it on his lap.

"Hands down as of right now, David Williams" James lied to the alien who sat down beside him politely. The top competitors as of now

383

were easily Max and Tesfa, but James had already decided anything but lying to these beings wouldn't result in any good.

"Really?" Yimb exaggerated the word. "He isn't even ranked top five among them and Max hasn't lost once to Catalina." Yimb pointed at the TV where Catalina and Max battled in hand-to-hand combat around a dark swampy battleground.

"Max isn't that great." James replied, "David hasn't been defeated in any match to Helen either."

"I wonder if you say this because you want to protect your American from the top placed champion chosen to represent the Federation." Yimb mocked him, and laughed humanly. James felt her eyes penetrate him. He turned to face her with a raised brow and a confused look then feigned that he didn't have any idea about how the rankings worked, though he did. "Well you already know each human will be given a new ranking when their training is complete," Yimb began to explain. At that moment, Roewle stepped out from the hallway and let out a gratifying yawn. James nodded his head, while still watching him come into the room. Last night when James had slept, he had a terrible dream about waking up to find the alien hunched over him. "Well each of their opponents will also be ranked," Yimb went on. James had already figured this much out.

"Will they be fighting with the SES?" James asked ignorantly.

"Yes," Yimb gave the obvious answer and began relaxing. James waited for more information, which she revealed; "All twenty of the first round competitors, ten humans and ten slaves, are given one week in the Realm of Rol to adjust to the modifications the SES provides."

Roewle sat next to him on the large flat cushiony piece of brown furniture and stared ahead at the monitor. It was hard for James to divert his attention from the strange alien. "So I'm assuming whoever is ranked first for the humans by the end of the training, will face off against whoever is ranked first from the ten slaves. Is that correct?" James asked awkwardly, unknowing what slaves were to the Federation.

"Yes. In the first round of the tournament, ten slaves have been chosen, all from Arghgripye," Yimb confirmed.

James looked at the television. From here, he would have to go out to the arena to find out everything he could about the tournament. Most of his time had been spent in the apartment sitting in silence with Yimb, watching the monitors. "Okay, I think I'm ready to go see the arena..." James glanced back over to Yimb, who returned his look with her furrowed forehead.

"Outstanding. I want you to meet someone special when we get there," Yimb calmly replied. They had only been in the city center near the massive arena once. It had been so crowded with so many alien species that he had gotten overwhelmed and Yimb had to get him back to the teleportation device.

They walked down Primary, the name of the street connecting hundreds of little shops with the massive high rises that rose up to the spacecraft's top. It was reminiscent of a downtown in a metropolis. James did his best not to look around the crowd they walked in, but a pink-skinned alien with humanoid eyes and yellow hair that stood taller than any man bowed its head slightly to him as they made eye contact. A childlike grey alien sold

387

smoking apparatus's on the corner to curious bystanders ranged from wide, to extra limbed, to hairy, to hairless. Every being that walked the black paved streets, like the humans in New York, were different. The pods flew overhead as they traveled on. It was hard adjusting from automobiles to the pods. It made James dizzy looking at them skitter by through the air.

"Fairoh, the biggest building in Arhgripye and second most important," Roewle clapped his hands together seemingly mesmerized when they approached the massive doughnut shaped building, too tall to see the top and too wide to see the sides.

"There's nothing in the galaxy like Fairoh's, The Realm of Rol, The Bylar Scanner, the Ritismic or Platform for that matter, Ambassador Coventry," Yimb informed him. As she took the lead, they approached the brown outer exterior of the building.

Two guardsmen, similar in height and clad in the battle armor stood at watch in front of a deserted great door. They saw Yimb approach and gave way. "Titan Yimb" one of the guardsmen nodded, recognizing her. Sliding to the side he continued "and Ambassador Coventry." He had recognized James as well. The three entered through the gate that peeled open slowly revealing a dark deserted corridor where paths were carved into the walls; it reminded James of a giant honeycomb.

"This is known as the Outer Ring. During the tournament these halls will be filled with slaves from across the galaxy," Yimb started as they walked around. It reminded James of being at the start of a concert or football game; in the biggest structure, he ever set foot. He looked up, unable to see a ceiling. "They will gamble on each match, purchase food or beverages, and watch the fights from one of the hundreds of recorders that will give a live feed," Yimb continued. It truly did sound like a sporting event.

"It's colossal" James commented. Yimb began to curve toward one of the many passages, which would seemingly lead them deeper into the area.

"Pharaoh! Pharaoh!" Roewle chanted as they walked.

Yimb led them into the corridor, but it ended much sooner than James had thought it would. They stood in a dark square room without a ceiling. "Titan Yimb" Yimb echoed and as she did, the computer's system responded to her. Firing up on the wall, its buttons began blinking and speaking in tones and dials. "Anti-gravitational reverse polarity activation," Yimb finished.

Aqua lights jetted up the walls and James felt his body become light, like a feather. "Whoa, what the..." James began to ask as he felt himself begin to gravitate in the air.

"Calm down," Yimb replied. He looked at her and Roewle who floated upward as well. He could feel his body begin to rise into the air. Roewle spun and clapped in amusement. "This type of transportation ensures that riff raff do not gain access to the Titans suites," Yimb explained as they floated up the square passage. They made it to another level of the building and James could finally see a ceiling. A gush of air propelled his body forward. He, Yimb, and Rowele landed on a soft black surface. As James looked ahead, the arena opened before them.

"The last time we were on Earth, the Arena hadn't even been thought of, so we hosted the tournament in many of Earths primitive cities. Entire populations bore witness to the humans that became godlike among their people," Yimb explained as they walked over to some observational seating toward the hollow arena. "After that tournament, Ra made some final adjustments." James stepped forward and made his way to the seating. The view opened up revealing the entire arenas battleground. It was very similar to a Roman coliseum, except there must have been seating that ranged in the millions. While the main stage where the competitors would do battle was only one football field wide, it was easily three times that in length. The dusky brown colored battleground floor sat darkened without lighting. James could imagine fierce humans having to fight for their lives against the monstrosities he had seen abduct them.

"One million will fill the seats and billions will watch live feeds. Those that cannot fit in seats crowd the outer rim. Those with a Titans status frequent these suites and will be able to view from a personal recorder or personal vision," Yimb went on.

"It will be unlike anything you have ever seen," Roewle commented in a forward, aggressive manner before James could say anything.

"I've noticed that with the SES weaponry the battles could easily harm the crowd..." James remarked, grabbing the wall that separated them from a ten-foot drop to another suite. Yimb sat down in one of the seats and sighed. The silvery metallic seating formed perfectly to her body. James sat in the seat next to her and once he did, he realized the metal molded itself underneath him, conforming to his exact weight.

393

"Oh!" Roewle stated gleefully leaping up onto the waist high barricade, "I can show you."

"Get down from there, Roewle" Yimb commanded, but the smaller alien didn't listen. Instead, it opened its mouth wide and made a vibrating noise. A beam of yellow light that began deep in his throat burst out toward the open arena floor. Before the beam got too far though, it seemed to stop only ten feet ahead of where they sat. Even though Roewle continued to shoot the beam out, it splashed and vanished against an invisible entity. Roewle closed his mouth and looked at James smiling. "Thank you, Roewle," Yimb sarcastically praised him for the dramatic demonstration as he jumped down and sat in the empty chair that conformed around his smaller body. "The most sophisticated defense system in all worlds, the Byra, is made from Ra's own spiritual energy. It doesn't allow anything to go in or come out of the arena, ever," Yimb said in her relaxed tone. James gave her a deep frown and put his hand on his chin, thinking. "There's something else I wanted to inform you James, the Federation has already captured several refugee's that were hiding away on your planet and using natural abilities to become famous and rich."

"What? There were aliens already living on earth?" Surprised by this, James responded quickly without thought. Yimb nodding confirming. James pulled it together attempting to cover his shock, he calmly said, "Well I can't say I'm surprised at this point." James left little time for pause and jumped right into his next question. "When will Ra make contact with Earth again?" Everything he thought, everything he said, had to be so precise, calculated.

395

"Random questions," Roewle said sternly, observing James with his curiously large eyes.

"Well, I would imagine there has been some kind of attempt at contact by the American people. As Ambassador, shouldn't I know these things?" James asked Yimb indirectly as he looked at Roewle. Roewle looked at James blankly, unknowing of what to say.

"The Chinese were infuriated," Yimb, answered honestly. James was taken aback, but didn't show any surprise. Not knowing how to react, he nodded his head slowly. "They, however, didn't react how Ra wanted them to," she finished. This part confused James.

"How Ra wanted?" James questioned her seriously; she sensed the change in his tone and made a stern face of her own.

"Yes." Yimb paused, as Roewle noticeably drew himself into the story, leaning over his chair and watching closely. "If it were up to Ra, he would exterminate every race in the galaxy."

"Why doesn't he just do that? I don't understand," James asked again.

"Traditions. The other Titans and the past champions won't allow Ra to break them" Yimb began explaining, "Ra will do everything in his power to make sure the humans lose this tournament. He will openly root against them in every match."

"I see" James observed. He sat back in the chair and rubbed his chin again.

"James Coventry, Ambassador to Earth. You don't see now, but you will." A deep, raspy, unfamiliar voice came from behind them. James spun in his chair and was astonished. He had expected to find another alien but instead he found another human being. The newcomer had brown skin and bushy black eye brows with peculiarly brown slanted eyes. Instead of the alien garb, he saw so many wearing what man wore an Egyptian ancient style cloth uniform. The golden and blue headdress was striped.

"Pharaoh!" Roewle shouted, launching itself up from the chair, he ran between the chairs and hopped forward embracing the man's leg.

"Hello, my little friend" the man patted Roewle on the head. Yimb rose to greet him, and so James followed suit.

"Pharaoh" Yimb acknowledged, looking at the man, she bowed her head in respect. By James' observation, she only did that to people that had a higher status than she did and she was directly connected to Ra, so had only been a few other of the Titans.

"Yimb" Pharaoh replied walking forward with Roewle still attached to his leg. The human gave Yimb a large embrace holding her tightly.

When Pharaoh retracted the embrace, he set his sights on James, and held out his hand.

"James Coventry, Ambassador to Earth," Pharaoh greeted him warmly. James instantly noticed the Pharaoh had a Xonotronic Translator.

"Yes" James nodded his head, shaking the Egyptian man's hand. "And you are Pharaoh?" James asked awkwardly. He hadn't dreamed a human would already be living here on platform, yet here he was, One of the winners of the last tournament on Earth, by what Yimb had said.

"Many planets, Solar Systems, light years ago; I lost my real name to time." Pharaoh responded, "I was one of two previous champions of the first tournament on Earth."

"Well, thank you and congratulations" James replied, releasing Pharaoh's hand.

"Thank you?" Pharaoh asked.

"Well, if it wasn't for you, humans would have been eradicated." James followed up informatively, "Would you mind telling me your story, and how you're still alive?"

"Ha, ha! It will take some amount of time," Pharaoh replied casually before taking the seat that Roewle had sat in. "James sit down." James followed orders and sat down, still curious about the Pharaoh's story; Yimb also sat while Roewle propelled himself onto Pharaoh's lap.

"In my days of fighting Ambassador, the tournament wasn't fought here on Platform; instead it was fought at the location of each Champion. A

400

monumental stadium was erected over seven days

by the slaves of Arhgripye." Pharaoh began

lecturing and held his hands up, palms outward

toward the arena. A green burst of energy shot out

from his hands, and the arena became a three

dimensional theatre. Pharaoh's spiritual power

created an illusion in the middle of the arena; a lone

human figure looking like a younger Pharaoh,

radiating green color lay in the center of the arena

floor, "I may not remember my real name, but the

tournament is something I can never forget."

Pharaoh continued, "I was abducted from my

people in the night by one of the ten chosen. When

I awoke in the desert and found the SES attached to

me, I thought my family had betrayed me and left

me to die." As he spoke, the human made from

Pharaoh's SES, so detailed and vivid, rose and

looked around as if lost. "And then a being

401

appeared to me who claimed to be from another planet, and explained the device attached to me. Before he left me there, he told me I had to face the greatest challenge of my life." Pharaoh swiped his hands easily, creating another being that seemed to talk to the young Pharaoh. James watched everything unfold before him; it was incredible enough that this man was still alive, but he seemed to have perfected control of his SES. The green tinted illusions seemed absolutely life like. "Little time passed. I wandered surviving off of any food I could find, and quickly managed to learn about the new power that rested in my hands," Pharaoh went on. The illusions on the arena floor turned into the Pharaoh fighting against a lion. The SES defended him well enough. After the lion was slain, the illusion feasted on its flesh over a fire.   "Then the alien being came back to me and took me to my

402

throne city, where a massive complex had been erected in my limited absence. My subjects had claimed the gods had arrived demanding that I fight as they watched." As Pharaoh went on James had the inclination Pharaoh carried strong resentment towards his people even after all this time had passed as he watched the illusions showing Pharaoh being dragged through the streets towards the stone arena door. "I fought and I won, three times" The illusions in the arena seemed to split and wage war against each other. Simultaneously aliens appeared and disappeared as Pharaoh landed a killing blow on each of them with a magical sword.

"Pharaoh! Pharaoh!" Roewle cheered, looking up at the much larger man.

"This arena and the concept of the tournament was built by the man you speak with," Yimb explained. "All of it was due to the ideas of

Master Pharaoh." Another twist, James thought. A human from Earth was one of the four Masters here on Platform.

Chapter 17: Security

The first day of training for Catalina had consisted of traveling to a place called the Murloy with Jazir, then the dueling with Max. He had beaten her every time but somehow she had been encouraged by him to push through all of it and to continue fighting. It was morning and they had rested after hunting together at night. Catalina laid there with her eyes open, hands under her head and dark hair like a pillow, watching the American boy sleep. This was the first time in years she hadn't been running away or acting in complete fear. The cartels and her government both wanted her dead. Fear had been the dominating factor in her life, so in turn she had become fear itself. They had nicknamed her the Black Widow after her second husband's death. Since that time, she had been on the run. Sex was her weapon, and stealing her crimes. Here right now, after dying fifteen times in one day, laying here in a remote swamp, next to the cute American boy, she felt safe. She began to wonder about his life and whom he really was which brought a smile to her face; she shut her eyes and dozed off once more.

"How are they?" Jazir asked Max and Catalina in her high-pitched voice, as they sat munching on the oval shaped pink fruit that their alien guide had brought. Catalina glanced up, but before she could speak, Max answered.

"It's great" Max replied, munching on another piece. "I can't believe these would grow in a place like this."

Catalina took another bite of the pink fruit as she watched Max chow. It had the texture of watermelon but tasted sweet and sour simultaneously, like a raspberry and a plum mixed. It was delicious and her body felt invigorated. She looked around the Murloy. It was so dark that even in the daytime it had stayed dark enough for her eyes to adjust. Her SES had worked superbly in the swamp. The dead trees and bushes that lined the watered grounds jutted up and permanently blocked out the artificial orange light, amplifying Catalina's newfound powers.

"Well, stand up. We don't have much time," Jazir rushed them both. Catalina rose as Max continued to munch. "Today I'll be giving you a personal lesson. Both of you relied heavily on melee capabilities during your first duels, which is fine," Jazir explained, as they stood in a far corner of the Murloy. "Today, we will learn how to punch."

"I know how to punch" Max spat out

ignorantly. Catalina gave him a quizzical look as he

arose and placed his hands across his chest,

standing firm. "Did you even watch us fight

yesterday? I didn't see you around."

"Of course I watched" Jazir commented.

"Max, what would you rather do than train?" The

female alien asked him. Catalina wondered the

same thing. Although Jazir wasn't similar to a

human being when it came to looks, she still

seemed quite feminine, especially when she spoke.

"I could just train on my own," Max blurted

out. Catalina felt her pride being injured.

"And you would just leave me?" Catalina

asked him scornfully, slapping his shoulder. He

reacted playfully as she knew he would. Even if

Max was as intelligent and strong as they came, he

was still a man that could be manipulated by her

girlish efforts. Catalina cowered and put on her best impression of pouty puppy dog eyes as she looked at him.

"No, I wouldn't leave you" Max replied to her romantically. Putting on a serious face, Catalina could make most men turn to putty by looking at them with those eyes. It was a power she didn't need her SES to use.

"Okay hot shot," Jazir interrupted the small moment between the two. "Let's make a little wager, Max."

"Okay, what type of wager?" Max asked the woman.

"Can't we just train, Max?" Catalina asked. She began losing patience, feeling frustrated with the American's behavior.

"No wait, I love betting, and I don't lose my bets," Max assured Catalina. She smiled slightly, enjoying the idea of a bet as well and Jazir seemed to have piqued his curiosity.

"I'll let you punch me as hard as you would like," Jazir explained motioning in the form of a punch.

"What?" Catalina asked in dismay. Jazir had a violent spark in her eye when she mentioned punching.

"Okay, then what?" Max asked.

"Then I'll hit you as hard as I want," Jazir continued, "Whoever hits harder, wins."

"What do we win?" Max asked interested in the prospect.

"If you win, I'll let you do whatever you want, with me and with her," Jazir motioned to Catalina, but before Catalina could protest, the alien continued. "You can do anything you want. I'll restrain her and submit to you."

410

"Wait stop" Catalina protested meekly. Her imagination began to run wild but it seemed to egg Max onward.

"Okay, I'll take that prize," Max intonated boldly, pointing at Catalina; Catalina couldn't help but smile again.

"In your dreams," Catalina teased, as Max walked up to Jazir.

"Ha, ha, you mean in your," Max laughed and teased her back. At that statement, she blushed and stayed silent. Had the man read her mind last night? It couldn't help but make her senses tingle as she watched him stand so rebellious.

"You will hit me first." Jazir challenged him planting her feet into the ground facing them. "Do not hold back, because I certainly won't."

"I won't hold back, I can't really tell if you are a lady or not, so no problem," Max now mocked

411

their guide, Jazir didn't smile however, and Catalina could read the seriousness on the female aliens.

"No matter how you look at it, I am female and you are male," Jazir mocked back, "Come and hit me you feeble piss ant."

"Feeble piss ant?" Were the last words Catalina could hear Max say before he disappeared into the air, his vanishing act wasn't invisibility or teleportation. Max moved at such high speeds Catalina was lucky to get a single hit on him in the duels.

Max didn't hesitate this time whatsoever, and Catalina couldn't see his movements they were so fast. He was in front of Jazir and wound up his balled up, hardened fist to land a devastating blow. The alien stood strong in place. Catalina watched his hand that should have clobbered Jazir like it had dozens of times to her. His thundering punch

412

smashed into Jazir's chest and let out a crackling thud, but the fury alien didn't budge. Instead, Max leapt backward and grabbed at his hand and cried out in pain.

Max groaned in agony as he grabbed at his wrist and hand. "What was that?" He yelled out, spinning in a super speedy circle as he grasped at his hand. His blue spiritual energy temporarily enshrouded from his elbow to his fingertips, healing the destructive damage that Jazir's presence had inflicted upon him.

"What happened?" Catalina blurted out in amazement. The female alien stood proudly, now looking at her.

"This is the difference between a fully adapted SES and that of an infant." Jazir extended her arms out as she walked forward and explained,

"If you let me teach you, you may have an opportunity to advance past the first round."

"That hurt" Max called out as he rose again. His hand had almost healed completely from his SES. His rejuvenation capabilities were what Catalina really envied. "But will you be able to move me?" Max taunted their guide again. Catalina watched as Jazir took on a resolved tone. In a split second, the alien dissipated, vanishing into the wind from their site. The female alien reappeared before Max and let out a ravenous war cry as she let loose a punch to his gut. Max flew back faster than Catalina could follow. His body bounced on the swampy surface, snapping trees and breaking full bushes apart. His body disappearing into the darkness Catalina felt slight relief and fright at seeing the man that had beaten her violently yesterday, manhandled so easily. While Catalina could already feel herself being attached to the American man, to see that Jazir was so powerful with a fully trained SES gave her hope.

"Well, I would like to learn from you," Catalina assured Jazir loudly, nodding her head. "Can you teach me how you did that?" she followed up.

"You will be able to do so much more child; I wanted him to know what it feels like to die." Jazir laughed after her last words. Catalina looked into the dark at where Max had flown into the swamp. Jazir didn't look like it, but she had the strength of ten men; hopefully, Catalina could take in the lessons and become just as powerful.

Max rubbed his head as he approached them from the dark and called out, "Well I guess you've won." As he got to them, Catalina could see the scarring on his chest begin healing. Jazir had blown a hole the size of Catalina's fist straight through his chest with her energy. A blue globe the size of his head circled electrically patching together the last remnants of his blown away skin.

Catalina watched as Jazir began what she called a conjuring, using SES and memory to create items from spiritual energy. Jazir stepped closer to them and lifted both of her hands to the sky. Although Catalina had seen some of the other guides abilities, she hadn't seen Jazir do anything but teleport, absorb and throw a punch. Appearing from the crevices of the Earth of the swamp, Jazir's lime green spiritual energy emanated upwards in a dozen places ten feet in height, and began spinning, forming many orbs. From within the dozen spheres, Catalina watched as Jazir moved her fingers rhythmically and large musky colored boulders the size of a small car formed in their places.

"That was incredible," Catalina complimented Jazir, who smiled back at her.

"These will be your dummies for now," Jazir explained after her creations were finished and her energy vanished.

Catalina punched again into the yellowish boulder with all of her might, her black spiritual energy burst as her fist connected with the rock. Nothing happened besides her fist flaring up in pain; she stepped back for a moment allowing the SES to heal her body with her energy. Max and she had begun punching the boulders repeatedly, but nothing had happened to them.

"Argh!" Catalina cried out as she punched into the boulder again. After she felt healed, Catalina muttered, "It is impossible!" The first time Jazir had shown them, she shattered the boulder into thousands of tiny pieces.

417

"Uaghhhh!" Max yelled out, as he put all of his weight into a punch. His boulder didn't budge, crack or move.

"The strength must come from within," Jazir hollered from behind them. "You must pull the power out of you."

"What does that even mean?" Catalina asked, wiping her brow.

Jazir walked forward behind Catalina, and put her large hand on Catalina's breast. Max watched with an interested look. "Your strength starts here, in your chest, where your organs are," Jazir began to lecture Catalina personally, whispering in her ear proactively and cupping her chest from behind. "That is where you draw your spiritual power from. You must feel it move from your chest, into your shoulder, down your arm and finally into your fist." As Jazir continued talking,

418

with each body part she mentioned, she grasped Catalina's firmly. Jazir took a step back and Catalina focused, first on her chest. She could feel the energy begin to form at the center, between her lungs. It radiated a warm feeling that quickly spread to her stomach; Catalina looked ahead at her target, the rock. She felt herself zone in on the area she would punch and cocked her fist back. The spiritual energy she was forming in her guts rushed up and she could feel it at her shoulder, as she whipped her fist forward for the straight punch, the energy zipped down her arm and into her fist. Her knuckles connected with rock, and a loud thud echoed into the air. Nothing happened. Catalina looked at the rock and let out a couple small breaths, it seemed like it would be impossible after all.

"I'm going to get it before you" Max gloated, smiling as he watched her; Catalina turned to him with a look of fury and determination.

"Humph, I wouldn't be so sure about that," Jazir barked. At that very moment, Catalina's rock cracked in a straight line where she had hit it; in an instant, the boulder splintered into millions of particle like pieces of debris that shot backwards in an explosive dust cloud.

"Holy crap." Max yelped. Even Catalina jumped back a little at the explosion she had caused.

"I did it," Catalina sighed. She looked from the obliterated boulder to Max, who looked back at her, "I did it!" In the heat of the moment, she felt herself launch across and Max met her half way. She embraced him in a victory hug; then quickly pulled away and containing her excitement, she stepped back looking at him embarrassed.

420

"I was just going to give you a high five but okay" Max joked with her which only made her skin flush.

"You saw what happened though," she said quietly.

"Yes, I did" Max responded nodding his head slowly.

"Well done Catalina," even Jazir was excited for her. "Now, there are fifteen more and you each have to smash them, so get to work."

"Maybe it would be best if you grabbed me like you were grabbing her," Max suggested jokingly. Jazir looked at him giving a small growl before turning around. "I'm just saying, maybe it will help."

Before they knew it, Catalina and Max shattered through two of the boulders. They celebrated by looking at one another with a smile.

Catalina made sure to keep her distance; being in this situation with Max made her feel secure, which in turn gave her more strength to continue.

Chapter 18: Interviews

"James, it's time we get going," Yimb, informed him as she walked up to the sofa he and Roewle sat on, watching the contestants. It has been five days total since the humans were dropped off in the Realm of Rol. Ra hadn't officially made contact with Earth; by James understanding, he and the three other Masters wouldn't meet the leaders until the 7th day of the contestants training, one day before the tournament began.

"Right, today we get to go into the Realm?" James asked again. It would be highly beneficial for him to meet each of the contestants. They had improved drastically over the last four days of basic training with their guides. Even Abdul had seemed to stop his hatred. Aishwarya had stopped complaining and Helen had accepted her duty for the continued prosperity of humanity. Each of them had a unique SES. Each of them seemed to handle the training differently.

"Shu!" Roewle yelped, smiling from ear to ear. James had seen Shu on the screen several times. According to all Yimb had shared the alien seemed to be one of the Masters, along with Ra and Pharaoh.

"Yes. Today you will get the opportunity to meet with some of the contestants to interview them," Yimb replied.

"Interview?" James asked. He hadn't even thought he would get to talk to them but now she was suggesting he interview them, probably while one of the invisible light recorders monitored.

"Yes. We want you to interact with some of the champions. As Ambassador to Earth, this will provide critical prescheduled entertainment prior to the airing of the tournament," Yimb explained.

"That would suit me just fine," James replied as he stood up to go. Today would be a critical day for them all.

Helen and David were training deep in the mossy jungles of Thoreinix, a segregated area in the Realm of Rol, for four days. Helen had been through it all. On the first day, she had fought David ten times and lost every fight. She was informed the Birk Modulator on her back wouldn't be with her in the actual tournament. On the second day, she and David both learned from their guide, Lazzea, how best to block incoming attacks. The dragon like alien launched hundreds of projectiles of pure energy at them that day until they could properly block every attack. The third day of training had consisted of learning how to attack.

The massive trees in the green covered jungle made perfect targets for both of them. Winding up the week of training consisted of more and more dueling. For their latest duel, they both fought Lazzea and badly beaten. As Helen reflected on the last few days, pressing herself tightly against one of the giant moss covered trees, David seemed to catch her wandering mind.

"Helen, you need to pay attention," David said to her gently. "If we don't work together, we will never be able to touch him."

Helen nodded a reply. As she did, Lazzea's raspy voice boomed out from behind the other side of the tree; "When you battle for your life in the arena, you will not be able to run and hide."

"Are you ready?" David asked her. She nodded her head again.

426

"I'll open; don't let me get hit this time,"
Helen replied boldly. She put her game face on;
this was a true test of how far she had come in the
last few days. Helen peeked around the tree seeing
the large alien and without hesitation sprung out
from the side of the tree. As she did, she formed
tiny white scalpel like projectiles launched
continuously at Lazzea as she moved acrobatically.
The alien turned in time to see her able to dodge to
the right. The white scalpels spun past his head and
body, barely missing. Now that Helen had his
attention, she wouldn't let up.

"There you are. Think you can hide from
me?" The alien coughed out, but Helen already had
released another salvo of the white scalpels, forcing
him to expand his wings in an attempt to take to the
air before they connected with his body, just as
David did in the first match when they both focused

427

on keeping a distance while firing projectiles.

Lazzea was a stern and intelligent guide, but Helen

had assumed he didn't expect them to ambush him.

She could see David's signature shark fin cutting

through the ground behind the massive alien, who

still had its attention focused on Helen. Right

before Lazzea could take to the air; David sprung

both hands up from the ground and held the alien

firmly using the earth as weight. At first Lazzea

looked down in confusion before looking up right in

time to see Helens attack connect with its massive

chest. As each one of the blazing white scalpels

connected with Lazzea's body, a ripping noise was

made. Briefly, the alien roared out in pain, but

Helen couldn't see any physical damage dealt.

Instead, Lazzea looked down at his legs where the

hands grasped on and focused energy from his

mouth.

428

"David let go!" Helen cried out, but it was far too late. Lazzea zapped the ground beneath him with an explosive bombardment of furious energy. From Helens view, a small nuclear blast had gone off and Lazzea vanished in the explosion. As it pushed outward, Helen was barely able to dodge behind one of the giant trees avoiding the blast taking her. Peeking around the corner of the tree Helen saw the smoke rise from the ground.

"One down, Helen" Lazzea yelled out from the center of the smoke. The words made Helen twinge.

She and David had both died many times in the last few days and each time it got harder to experience. Quickly Helen came up with an off the top of her head plan; peeking out at the smoke again, she decided to go for it. She could feel herself sprint out into the mist and could see

Lazzea's massive body looking around for her. That meant David was still there; he hadn't moved. Using her SES to propel herself forward like a bullet from a gun, Helen slid on the smooth green ground, right toward Lazzea's feet. Propelling herself faster, skirting into a baseball slide, and just about to pass Lazzea, Helen was able to grab one of David's dead hands out of the ground. Feeling the extra weight, with both of her feet she concentrated the spiritual energy in the opposite direction. Stopping her body right under Lazzea who managed to look down at her just in time to see her direct the flow of energy into her arm and fling a lifeless David up and out of the ground, over through the trees.

"What is this?" Lazzea asked, startled that she had made it so close without him noticing. For a mere second, she watched on the ground as he

430

began to build up yellow spiritual power in his open mouth to zap her as he had David. Promptly she focused the SES's powers and flew backwards. "What makes you think I'll let you get away?" Lazzea roared as he released the bright yellow explosive from his mouth. It trailed Helen closely. Realizing she wouldn't be able to outrun the yellow ball, Helen put one hand out and pushed hard, bursting out some of her white spiritual energy diverting the angle of the approaching danger. The yellow explosive flew by her head and hurled into one of the massive trees behind her, exploding on impact. The boom echoed a supersonic blast that only accelerated Helens speed away propelling her from the creature. Just like before during training, Helen was able to gain her composure, recover, and regaining her footing she sprinted away from Lazzea into the green of the jungle.

431

It only took her a couple minutes to reach

the corpse of David. The thing about the Birk

Modulator, they worked in pairs, utilizing the

spiritual energy inside to self-repair any type of

damage, but David's wouldn't work until Helen died

and Lazzea was declared the winner. Helen lifted

his head; he was still breathing. "Oh well done!"

She said. Putting both of her hands out to heal him,

a white mist swallowed David's burnt body and his

skin began to regenerate. If she could restore him

to new with her SES, they still had a chance at

beating Lazzea. David's indented head had taken the

brunt of Lazzea's attack, and it began to balloon out

as his skull rebuilt itself. Helen recalled and

captured what the Birk Modulator had done to

David's body the first time she saw him comeback

from the dead, and replicated the effect with her

SES.

432

David was healed fully. He gasped for air and looked up at her as the healing mist evaporated upwards. "So, I'm guessing our first attempt didn't go as planned?" David asked her. She frowned, confirming his suspicions.

"Well then, on to plan B" Helen suggested. David now smiled as he sat upwards.

"Little brats! You will not have time for a plan B!" Lazzea roared, as he appeared from the sky, landing gracefully next to them, his multicolored wings folding up against his back. Helen looked at him but still could react; she hadn't recovered enough from the expenditure of energy. She checked out David who was trying to move; he hadn't recovered either. Lazzea already had the yellow bomb forming in his mouth when he began speaking. As he released it, Helen prepared herself to be blown away, along with David. The yellow ball traveled slowly across the green colored atmosphere of the jungle. Just before it was about to make contact another voice stormed out from the jungle; a voice Helen hadn't heard before.

"That is enough, Lazzea!" the voice commanded. Obeying his master, Lazzea quickly teleported positioning himself in front of Helen and swallowed the yellow explosive.

"Titan Yimb" Lazzea scoffed the name letting out an alarmingly loud burp as he turned to Helen and David's' side and greeted the new voice. Helen followed the direction here Lazzea was looking and saw the new arrivals walking toward them through the trees. One of them was a feminine alien with multicolored patterned skin wearing feminine pink silk robes that sprawled out and trailed her as she led the group. The next was a small being, only a few feet in height, he waddled closely to the female; his big eyes perched on his head observing all of the wonders in the jungle. The last was a male human, adorned in protracted red and black silky robes that gave him the appearance of a wealthy monk. The man stared ahead at David and Helen in awe; she returned the look having no idea who he was.

"David, Helen," the man called out as the three of them approached. Their green shaded bodies became further detailed as they approached and the man spoke again. "My name is James Coventry," he introduced himself. Helen didn't know how to react to the man, and by the looks of things, neither did David.

"He was chosen by the people of Earth to be Ambassador for your planet," the female alien explained. Lazzea kept his head bowed toward the female alien. "I am Yimb. This is my companion

Roewle," she pointed at the strange looking, smaller being.

"Howwwwwdddddyyyyy." Roewle waved his hand over his head and extended out the word.

"Hello. What is your name little guy?" Helen asked. It was the first time she had been amused for days. David seemed rigid an on edge; on top of it he didn't talk much to her, as if he had been hiding something. Roewle was a delightful treat.

"Roewle" he yelled delightfully. Walking up to Helen, the small alien hugged her leg. "You are so pretty." Helen looked to David, who didn't seem to care but instead focused on James.

"You're even more beautiful in person, Helen," James commented. David frowned but Helen took the compliment kindly, "And David you've been flawless fighting."

"What is your exact role, Ambassador?" David asked him.

"David, do not address your Ambassador with such disrespect." Lazzea barked at David, who cringed at the thought of angering the alien guide. Helen chose to walk up to shake his hand.

"Pleasure to meet you, Ambassador" Helen greeted him cautiously.

"You must be pretty shocked by this entire experience Helen. Please stand vigilant." James continued.

Yimb seemed to take charge of the conversation. "Lazzea, you have had them for five days. Tomorrow is the time for them to get their battle armor and we leave from here to rendezvous with Shu," Yimb announced to the group.

"Well then, they are as prepared for the next two steps in their training as they will ever be,"

437

Lazzea replied. Helen was almost flattered by the prospect of them being ready but it seemed like a lie. When they had fought their guide, they had barely harmed him.

"Battle armor?" David asked out to Yimb, who had brought the subject up. It broke Helens' thoughts.

"Like the aliens that abducted us wore?" Helen thought aloud. It wasn't the first time she had made an acute observation and impressed Lazzea.

"Yes Helen, how keen of you." Yimb purred the words out with a subtle undertone of intimidation. After doing so, James seemed to give the alien an offended look and she lost the attitude.

"Well then, shall we get going?" Lazzea interrupted the moment of tension.

Chapter 19: Battle Armor

Each of the contestants sat looking at each other at the table in the Hall of Shu. It had felt like forever to David. He looked down at his fingertips. His SES had sunk deeper into his hands, virtually becoming translucent vein lines in his skin. The earthly food they had consumed, steak, potato, cheeses, wine, cake, none of it replenished his body like the food he and Helen had scavenged deep in the jungles. David finally tuned joining the conversation, which was taking place at the table. All of the contestants, Abdul and Aishwarya included, seemed to have accepted this was inevitably their fate and to save humanity they would have to fight. All of them but Abdul laughed as Bai continued talking about his time with Aishwarya.

439

"I swear!" Bai laughed out the words as he grabbed Max tightly by the shoulder, "I said move damn you Aishwarya and she moved right into the fireball!" David chuckled as Tesfa across from Bai lost his marbles in laughter. The women more so giggled at Tcsfa's astonished reaction to the jokes because the man clearly didn't handle his wine well. James Coventry, who sat at the opposite end of the table in the chair that had been vacant last time, joined in on the conversation.

"Well, what happened next?" James asked, while slicing some of the meat on his plate with a small laser knife.

"What does it matter what happened next!" Abdul violently interjected from his corner of the table. Shu had warned them earlier he wouldn't tolerate any violent behavior or actions among them, but already Abdul had burst out like this twice.

"Oh lighten up buddy! We were telling a story!" Lucya mused next to him, slapping Abdul hard on the back. The entire table went silent for a moment as they watched Lucya who took a large gulp of the wine, realizing that she may have been out of line. Abdul looked at her in confusion. Whether it was because she was a beautiful woman, or because Shu had threatened them, he managed to hold his tongue.

"So, what happened? Continue." Tesfa urged Bai to get back to the story with his big opened eyes.

Bai paused getting back into the moment and glanced over to the young Indian woman. "I got arrogant." Bai admitted. At that moment, everyone's attention was fixated on him. Even Shu

441

at the end of the table, who had let them badger

each other and talk freely, seemed to listen intently.

"Aishwarya was able to ambush me, and took my

life," Bai depressingly admitted to the group.

"Ha, ha, ha, ha!" Tesfa laughed, breaking

the silence. "We all died!" Tesfa blurted out. The

rest of them joined in the laughter as well. Even

David found Bai's theatrics and Tesfa's reactions

amusing. It was a true statement, they had all

experienced death with the Birk Modular's attached

to their backs, but those were gone now, taken by

the guides as they entered the hall of Shu. David

looked over at Helen who had participated in the

conversation and giggled alongside Catalina, the

beautiful Mexican woman. Helen, his training

partner, had managed a near replication of the effect

of the Birk Modular in just a matter of a few days.

The SES amplified her medical prowess and the

woman could heal herself just as fast as she took damage. It seemed as though immortality was in her grasp. David looked at her in envy and she returned his gaze smiling. Raising her glass, she took a sip of the wine.

"Shut up you idiot" Abdul tried scolding Tesfa again from the end of the table. Everyone else became quiet again at his negativity. "Don't you realize how unholy you sound in his ears?"

"Listen pal..." Max began, but Tesfa held his hand up, interrupting the American who looked at Abdul with disconcert.

"Abdul, you are angry because you are losing your faith." Tesfa obnoxiously scoffed at the Middle Eastern warrior who was immediately riled by the words. "I know my god, I know my faith, and I know he will watch over me." Tesfa went on. With each word, Abduls face cringed but the man kept his mouth shut. Again, Shu was giving him an intense stare.

"This is a hard situation for everyone," Max tried diplomatically handling Abduls anger. "No one asked to come here and play hero." As Max continued talking, it seemed to sober up the room. Everyone, including David, began to think about the magnitude of the situation.

"It's going to be a fight to the death," the Ambassador humbly said, looking up from the food at his plate.

"When do we learn more about tomorrow?" Aishwarya asked Shu. The giant white alien at the end of the table put down a bowl and utensil he had used to eat a red alien paste.

"Tomorrow..." Shu thought for a moment, "Tomorrow, early in the morning, you will each be

444

teleported to a different section of a place in this realm called the Zipphire."

"Another strange battleground" Max asked, "How big is this place?"

"Much bigger than you could imagine," Catalina jokingly sassed him; he looked back at her and gave the woman a playful shove. David had noted that the two had seemed to form a bond like he and Helen had over the course of training. Although they were forced to hurt each other, they were doing it to learn.

"The Zipphire is not one of the ten battlegrounds here in the realm," Shu remarked in a grave voice. It gave David a chill down his spine that traveled all the way down to his knees. "The Zipphire is one of the most dangerous places in the Realm," the host of the Realm added, only increasing the danger level David felt.

445

"And why are we going here again?"
Aishwarya asked in a serious tone. David had the
impression she still resented having to be there.
Even if we didn't have a choice in the matter,
Aishwarya seemed like the type of woman that
would protest.

"You will be divided; each of you will scour
The Zipphire for your piece of battle armor that will
help you in various ways," Shu replied.

"That's pretty vague," Helen, piped up.
"How is the battle armor beneficial to us when we
already have the SES?"

"It's part of the tradition of your training,
just like your spiritual mentor, and the body armor
will help you absorb damage during the tournament.
Trust me, even the best of you at this table will get
hit" James answered; he kept a steady focus on Max
for a second before scanning the others.

446

"I see Yimb has informed you well, Ambassador." Shu replied to the information that James already possessed.

"Yes; well, for five days they've trained and for five days I've learned everything I can," James curtly responded to Shu who smiled slyly. David noticed how diplomatic James Coventry was and wondered who the man had been on Earth. To be selected for such a position, he would have to be very important.

"Well, has everyone finished their meals?" Shu asked loudly to the room. Everyone seemed to agree and finished eating; Tesfa took another big gulp of the wine. Looking down at James, Shu said, "The Ambassador will conduct brief interviews with each of you."

"Interviews" Bai asked sharply.

447

David had waited at the table for an extended amount of time. First Abdul had been called in, then Catalina, and now Max. Although Catalina and Abdul had been balanced in time, James Coventry and Max had been in the room for an extended period. David looked at the door to the room wondering where the others went after their interview. As if reading his mind, Helen spoke out.

"Where did Catalina and Abdul go, Shu?" Helen asked. Before David could hear the answer, the door opened and James popped his head out.

"David Williams." James announced his full name before his head fell back into the room and the door slid closed. Shu never answer the question. David looked at the others, stood from the table and made his way to the electric double door that separated open. Slowly David entered the room and the door shut closed behind him. Inside the small

448

mostly white room was a yellowish wooden desk
and two chairs the same as those they sat at around
the dinner table. James sat in one behind the desk
motioning for David to join him, "Come, and sit
down." David made his way down into the
comfortable white chair in contrast with the wood
desk and the stiff grey walls. "So, David Williams"
James crossed one leg over the other and cusped his
knee. "Where are you from?" At first David, didn't
know how to react to the question; he sat back in his
chair and crossed his arms.

"You're going to act like the rest of them
too?" David asked James. James gave him a
puzzled look without replying. "Listen, I know there
is a recorder in this room. I don't care." David
stated suspiciously and in anger toward James
silence. He looked behind his chair and up into the
corners of the room. "You should be giving all of

us any helpful information you can." For a second it seemed as though James contemplated telling him to piss off. He looked at him and rubbed one of his ears. The alien robes made him look like a disco infused rabbi swayed with his fingers movements.

"Okay, why don't we just answer some basic questions to start out with?" James suggested with a raised brow. David chose not to argue. "So where are you from then David?" James repeated the question.

"I'm from Gold Coast, Australia." David hurried the answer.

"And how old are you David?" James asked quickly.

"I'm twenty five years old." David answered.

"Okay excellent." James responded, "And, how are you handling this entire situation?" James inquired.

David looked back at him puzzled, "What do you mean?" David buzzed feeling uncomfortable about answering truthfully.

"That recorder is no longer recording us for the time being." James whispered, pointing with one hand in the corner next to the door. The Ambassador held his other hand up for a moment and clutched something in his fingers. David assumed it was a tiny piece of an Xhorni particle; it was a small piece of crystal with an appearance similar to a red rose bud. "They call it an Xhorni Particle" James mused with David, having a small laugh. "I could only steal a small chunk of one, so I'm breaking it up among a few of you." David laughed. It was the first genuine laugh he had since being on Earth with his cousin.

"So, who are you?" David asked bluntly, calming himself and setting back into the serious mood James Coventry carried.

"My name is James Coventry. I'm a special agent with the United Nations and I'm in charge if anything like this ever happens" James answered.

"So, you really are just a diplomat." David chuckled, but James was serious as ever.

"David, what I'm about to tell you may change everything for better or for worse" James dared. David felt himself get tense as he prepared for any information to help him in the tournament. "No matter the results of the tournament, I don't think Ra is going to leave Earth unscathed. I believe that he has every intention of exterminating human kind from the planet, utilizing this space ship." James concluded. It was so quiet in the room; one could hear a penny drop from miles away.

452

"Do the others know?" David asked. "Are you telling the others this same thing?"

"No." James replied dully rubbing his chin and staring back at David without blinking.

"Why?" David asked, but before he answered, James held one finger up with the hand that wasn't holding onto the particle.

"We've run out of time." James quickly stated, "So what do you do for a living?" James continued the interview; David looked up where the Light Recorder hovered invisibly in the corner of the room. The interview was over in a short time. David had answered all of James's generic questions but his mind hadn't lingered from the obvious, these aliens were going to try to destroy Earth. David got up from his seat while James extended a hand out to him; they shook firmly.

"I'm sorry you're in the situation you're in, but you seem strong David. You will be okay." James imparted the words onto him before David turned to exit by the door. "No, not that way," James cut him off before he could fully turn around and David turned back toward him. "That wall right there," James pointed, David looked to where he was directing. It wasn't anything he had noticed earlier by just glancing around the room, but the wall flickered like a mirage.

"Where does it go?" David asked James wearily. He had an uneasy feeling about it.

"Each Champion will be teleported to the edge of The Zipphire. There will be instructions for you when you get there" James replied, putting his hand on David's shoulder. David allowed James to guide him across the room, and without looking back, he walked through the translucent wall.

454

When he arrived on the other side, it was unlike the scenery he had witnessed before in the desolate swamp. A small camp with a tent and fire were already set up for him in a tiny patch of clearing. Surrounding the camp were giant darkly shaded trees that swayed up into a sublime black swirling with aqua green sky. David made his way over toward the small fire where one chair sat near the edge of the heat. Taking a seat, he watched the orange flickering flames dance along the dark sky. Listening to his surrounding, David could hear unknown animals call out to each other in the night. Still, he thought it would do as he took to the tent for some sleep.

"Get up!" David heard a familiar voice yelling outside of the tent the next morning. David got himself composed and looked out the tent. It was Serta, one of the guides. David opened his eyes

455

wider from the attempted slumber he had put on himself. With all of the wild animals roaring and crying out, he hadn't been able to sleep well. The sky hadn't changed at all. The trees were still shaded. The Realm of Zipphire was truly a dark place. "It is time David, for you to get your battle armor," Serta announced. "You have until the remainder of the day, to find your piece of armor and make it back to the hall of Shu. Best of luck!"

"Wait, how am I supposed to know how to get back?" David asked, but Serta's body was twisting and disappearing into the dark canvas, leaving things as if he was never there in the first place, Serta teleported out. "Well, that's fantastic" David commented to himself. Pulling his weight out of the tent, he walked over to where Serta stood moments ago noticing the small dying fire and observed the area again. In each direction, a small path cut into the woods. "This is the only time I'll get to try this out." David spoke aloud to himself again. He thought of the idea while fighting Helen but didn't get the opportunity to use it. Now was the perfect opportunity for David to try sonar. He could get a location on the other contestants and possibly a big hunk of armor metal in woods like this. David walked forward to the first clearing, and relaxed himself. Raising both of his arms and pointing his fingers outwards, he focused all of the power in the SES. Two purple rings formed in the palms of his hands and putting his strength behind a push, David closed his eyes tight and lunged one leg forward. The two rings expanded outward becoming larger as they moved out into the woods, leaving a trail of smaller translucent purple rings. David waited in anticipation not knowing if it was going to work. He could feel both the primary rings,

457

as if he was traveling with them through the alien laced jungle at super speeds; multicolored leaves and dusky brown floor spin as his spirit zipped past causing a gush of wind. Then, the ring on the right collided into something that was breathing. Both of the rings warped back through time and space causing a forceful current of air and even the mightiest of plant life swayed. David held up his hand; as the rings got closer, they shrunk in size and made a loud plop as he absorbed them both back into his hands. David could see Bai standing by his own tent as if he was right next to him. Bai looked as if he was reacting out of paranoia and quickly scorched a tree in David's direction. "Hmmm." David contemplated to himself, turning around he headed for one of the other paths. "Better not go that way," he chimed, stepping ahead to the other side of the tiny campground.

458

Holding his hands up, he repeated the process. The rings zipped out deep into the jungle, and once again made contact, this time with two people. David waited anxiously to see what was happening as the sonar traveled back to him. As it reached his hands, he could see clearly, Aishwarya was already traveling through a portion of large fallen over trees and rocks. Abdul was stalking slowly not even twenty yards behind her.

459

Made in the USA
Middletown, DE
23 May 2016